Moonflower

A Halloween Novella

Elira Firethorn

To all the ones who understand that sometimes,
the smut is *the plot.*

Playlist & Storyboard

Playlist:

Liar – Magnolia Park
Boom-Boom-Boom – Rob Zombie
Everything is Changing – Saint Middleton
Pieces of You – nothing,nowhere.
I'll Give You The Stars – Magnolia Park, fats'e, TITUS
Darkness At The Heart Of My Love – Ghost
Now Or Never – Meet Me @ The Altar
Hunter's Moon – Ghost
Send in the Machines - Bohnes

Storyboard:
You can view Moonflower's storyboard at
pinterest.com/elirafirethorn

Before You Read

Moonflower is an erotic novella intended for readers over the age of 18.

It touches on depression (including apathy and suicidal ideation), feelings of unworthiness, a mention of disassociation, and anxiety. There's also swearing, a fear of domestic violence, kicking someone (not one of the main characters) out of their home, and violence against a person (not one of the main characters).

It includes explicit sex scenes that have uninformed consent (one scene), fear play, primal play (chasing), CNC (consensual non-consent, which in this case includes threat of murder), spitting, breath play, degradation/humiliation, pain play, wax play, marking/bruising, choking, over-stimulation, sensory deprivation (blindfolding), and domination/submission.

The scenes in this book aren't meant to be a guide to BDSM or kink. This is a work of *fiction*.

MOON FLOWER

Chapter One

Cora

Note: This book contains some darker themes/kinks. Please flip back and read the Before You Read section if you haven't already.

Two weeks before Halloween

Nothing has the power to ruin your day like realizing you've fucked everything up. Royally and irrevocably. And nothing will make that gut-wrenching feeling hit harder than sitting on your bed and staring at your wall of photos of you and your best friends.

My heart aches as I survey the section that's full of pictures of the three of us dressed in Halloween costumes and laughing at the camera. The photos start young—when we were all five years old—and go all the way through our senior year of high school.

Sighing, I take down the last picture I have of the three of us, brushing my fingers over their faces. We're all grinning at the camera, happy and naive. It was the day they helped me move into this apartment at the beginning of my freshman year of college.

Before I realized I couldn't pretend anymore.

Before I stopped letting myself dream.

Before I ruined everything.

Ezra and Wilder. They stayed in our hometown for school, and I moved to Philadelphia to attend Westview University. It gave me the distance I needed to get over my stupid fantasies. Well, that was the plan, anyway.

As if my thoughts summoned them, my phone buzzes. When I grab it, I see Ezra's grinning face staring up at me from the screen.

I accept the video call, plastering on a convincing smile. Ezra appears, his brown curls falling into his pale face. It's been a couple months since I've seen him—we've mostly just texted or done normal phone calls.

"Hey, Moonflower," he says with his signature heart-melting smile. "How's it going?"

My fingers curl into a fist all on their own, crumpling the edge of the picture I'm holding. *Shit.* I let it fall to the bed. "I'm good. Overwhelmed with homework, but what's new, right?"

He groans. "Yeah, I get that."

"You . . . uh. You grew out your hair." I peer down at my screen, trying to get a better look at him. It's been almost half a year since I've seen him in person, and the realization makes the ache in my chest grow.

Ezra's smile falters. "You don't like it?"

"I . . ." My mouth goes dry. It's not that I don't like it. It's that I *love* it. And currently, my only thought is of threading my fingers through his soft curls while he has his head in between my legs.

Ever since we were teens, I've wanted both Ezra and Wilder. It's a selfish thing—one I know neither of them would go with. And there's no way I can choose between them.

So I left. I came here for college, found myself a boyfriend, and tried to move on. My plan has failed miserably—I can't get either of them out of my head—but what am I supposed to do? If I can't have both of them, I can't have either of them.

"Does it look bad?" Ezra asks. "I can cut it."

"Oooh, let me try," Wilder says mischievously somewhere off-screen.

I shake off a shiver. "No, I like it. It looks cute."

With a frown, Ezra says, "Cute? Like a little kid?"

"No! No, like . . ." My voice is too high-pitched, so I pause to take a calming breath. "It looks hot."

"Oh."

Silence. Then Wilder appears on the screen, pushing Ezra out of the way. His summer tan has mostly faded, and his dark hair is still styled the way it always is—short but still long enough I could run my fingers through it.

"You've never called Ezra hot before."

"I've never called *either* of you hot before." *It's too close to the truth.*

Wilder pouts, sticking his bottom lip out the way he used to do all the time when we were kids.

With a laugh, I say, "Fine, fine. You're hot too, Wild."

He gives me a satisfied grin before Ezra grabs his phone, coming back into view. "Everything going okay? Friends? You and Matt?" He says the last part more quietly, almost like he's . . . jealous? That can't be right.

"Friends are good. We're thinking of going on vacation together this summer. Me, Brooke, Liling, and Imani, that is."

"That sounds cool," Wilder says, shoving his face right next to Ezra's. "Kinda fast, though. Haven't you only been friends with them for a couple months?"

"I mean, we were on each other's radars before."

"You trust them?"

"Of course, Wilder."

"Dude," Ezra says. "Chill out."

"I'm allowed to be cautious! Our little Moonflower can be too trusting sometimes. Speaking of being too trusting, how's Matt?"

I brush off his comment with an eye roll. "Fine, I guess. He'll probably be home soon from hanging out with the guys."

"I thought tonight was supposed to be date night," Ezra says. "That's what you told me yesterday."

"Plans changed." I shrug.

Wait. If he knew tonight was date night, then why did he call me?

Wilder and Ezra exchange a loaded look. My heart sinks.

"You knew he'd cancel, didn't you?"

Ezra grimaces, and Wilder clenches his jaw.

"There's a pattern, Cora. Don't know how you don't see it." Ezra's expression is one of deep discomfort. He runs a hand through his curls.

"I know," I mutter.

To be honest, things haven't been that great with Matt and I for a while. We started dating at the beginning of our junior year, and we decided he should move in with me this semester. Ever since, things have gone downhill.

Well . . . not that there was ever an *up*.

"You know you're settling with him, right?" Wilder's tone is serious. Maybe even a little annoyed.

I sigh. Of *course* I know I'm settling. But I can't have what I really want. It's selfish. And a potential recipe for disaster.

"Cora," he says again with a hint of impatience.

"I can handle my own love life," I say.

Wilder looks like he's about to say something snarky, but Ezra cuts him off.

"We know. We just don't want you to get your heart broken."

I laugh. It's more bitter than amused. Because the two men on the other side of my screen are the only ones who hold the power to break my heart.

"It's not funny, Cora," Wilder grits out.

"I'll be fine," I say, forcing lightheartedness into my voice. "You two worry too much."

"Worry too much?" Wilder snaps. "Cora! This is your *wellbeing* we're talking about. We're your best friends. What's going to happen if he breaks up with you out of the blue? You're going to be all alone, and then you'll start avoiding us again, and then you'll—"

"Wild, she has other people she can rely on," Ezra says.

"But *we're* her best friends." Wilder glares at me through the phone. "We're the ones who should take care of you."

I sigh. That right there is why I know I can never have both of them. Wilder is too possessive. There's no way he'd be willing to share me with Ezra—if he even wants me. And there's no way I can date Ezra *without* being with Wilder. It would hurt too much.

"What are you even suggesting?" I ask.

"Break up with him."

"What?!"

"You're fucking *miserable*, Cora. You think you're hiding it well. But you forget how well we know you."

Ezra nods, humming in agreement.

"I . . ."

Shit. They're right. I know they're right. I got together with Matt to get my mind off these two. When we started dating, we both liked each other, but at this point we're no good together. That's the thing, though. I'd rather be miserable and distracted than miserable with nothing to keep my thoughts occupied.

I'm not sure why Matt has stuck around. Maybe because I'm his ticket to cheap rent? Because he doesn't have to clean up after himself? It's definitely not the sex—we haven't had any in at least a month.

Ezra must sense my mood souring, because he switches the subject. "You excited for Halloween, Moonflower?"

Fuck. We always spend Halloween together. The past couple years, I haven't been able to come home because I've had classes the morning after. This year, Halloween is on a Friday, but I wasn't planning on coming home. I can't be around them. Not without my mind spiraling out of control.

"Um . . . yeah."

There's a slight pause. Ezra's smile wavers. "You're coming home, right?"

Silence. My heart practically rips in two as I take in Ezra's broken expression.

Wilder jumps straight to anger. "You *promised* us you'd come back."

"I'm just . . . really overwhelmed. With school."

Ezra shoves Wilder, and his expression softens. His jaw is still clenched tightly, though.

"Imani and DeAndre are throwing a Halloween party at their house," I say. "I'm going to that with the girls. I just don't think I can manage the drive home. It's a lot of time, and I'm behind on homework, and I—"

"Don't," Wilder says. "You don't have to explain yourself. I get it. Sorry I snapped."

"Is there anything we can do to help you, Moonflower?" Ezra asks.

I shake my head. "No. But thank you."

The sound of the front door opening and closing drifts into my bedroom. Matt must be home.

"I should go," I say.

"Got it. Love you, Cora," Ezra says.

"A lot," Wilder adds.

"Love you guys too," I reply quietly enough Matt won't hear.

I hate hanging up on them, but I do it anyway. If Matt catches me talking to them, he'll go on a rant about how I care more about them than I care about him. Which is *true,* but it's ironic considering he doesn't prioritize me.

Maybe I should break up with him.

No. I need the distraction.

"Cora?" he calls.

"In here," I say, picking up the picture I dropped. As I stick it up on the wall again, Matt comes in.

"Oh, are you finally taking that shit down?"

I freeze, thumbtack in hand. "What?"

"The pictures of you and those two. You taking them down?"

"Why would I do that?"

"You hardly see them anymore. Barely talk to them."

Barely talk to them in front of you.

"I'm not taking them down. They're my best friends."

Matt rolls his eyes and leaves. Typical.

I resume staring at the pictures of me and the boys for a few minutes. It only worsens my mood and makes me wish for things that'll never happen.

For me to not be so damn selfish. For Wilder to not be so possessive. For me to be okay with being just friends with him and Ezra.

"Wishing won't get you anywhere, Cora," I mutter.

A distraction—that's what I need. A shower and then something to keep my thoughts off Wilder and Ezra.

In the bathroom, I pull back the shower curtain to turn the water on. Then I grimace. I asked Matt to clean in here earlier, and I swear he did. I smelled the cleaning chemicals and everything. So why is the shower still dirty?

Stepping back from the shower, I take in the rest of the bathroom. Now that I'm actually looking, *most* of it doesn't look clean.

"Hey, Matt?" I call.

"What?" It takes a second, but then he appears in the doorframe, arms crossed.

"Did you . . . did you clean in here?"

"Yeah." He raises an eyebrow, like he knows exactly where this conversation is about to go.

"But it's not clean."

"It is."

"There's still soap residue on the shower walls. And it looks like you didn't even sweep." *Or clean the sink.*

He peers into the bathroom. "Looks fine to me."

"But it's—"

"If you're going to be so nitpicky, maybe you should've done it yourself."

I clench my fists. "I'm not being *nitpicky.*"

Matt rolls his eyes. "You're just like my mom. All you do is nag."

"Matt!"

"Whatever. I'm going to bed." He heads into our room and shuts the door harder than he needs to.

I sigh, re-cleaning the bathroom, which only pisses me off even more. All I want to do is distract myself with one of the shows I'm currently watching.

Once the water is warm, I step under the spray. Immediately, my mind goes to Ezra and Wilder. What would it be like to shower with one of them? With both of them?

I glance down at my round stomach and ample thighs. There's no way we could be together in *this* shower. It's too small, especially considering Wilder and Ezra have both towered over me since we were young teens. Combined with their ridiculously broad shoulders from working out all the time, this thing is just too small. But maybe in a bigger shower . . .

Stop. Just stop, Cora. That'll never happen.

I finish scrubbing myself clean and then dry off and put my favorite lotion on. After getting dressed, I settle on the couch in the living room, ready to relax, but I find myself scrolling through my shows. None of them seem appealing.

Maybe I should try journaling.

I look around for a notebook for a minute, but then I realize I'm not sure I want what's on my mind written out on paper. What if Matt snoops through my stuff or finds it by accident? That definitely wouldn't end well.

Settling on the couch again, I grab my laptop and pull up my old blog. It used to be my own sort of journal when I was a kid. I'd post shitty poems, pictures I took, and whatever thoughts were running through my head.

I made my blog private my sophomore year of high school, so no one has access to it. It's the perfect place to rant without having to worry about someone reading it. And maybe if I can write out my feelings about Matt, and then the jumble of thoughts I have about Ezra and Wilder, I'll feel better.

"It's worth a try," I mutter, hitting the button to create a new post.

And then I start typing.

Chapter Two

Wilder

One week before Halloween

I groan when my phone vibrates on my desk. Texts, DMs, emails, notifications—sometimes it's just too fucking much. My senior year of college has already proved to be exhausting enough. Having my phone go off every twenty minutes only adds to the stress.

There are only two people in this world I consistently message back and forth with—Cora and Ezra. I rarely reply to anyone else unless it's important. Still, avoiding my notifications is a recipe for disaster. If I let messages sit for too long, I end up ignoring them for weeks. So I abandon the article I'm working on and check my phone.

Mom: Did you get my e-mail?

Wilder: I never check my email.

Mom: Found a job I think you'd like. Pays well.

I roll my eyes. Of course she did.

My parents both want the best for me. I get that. It's endearing, honestly. But it's also annoying as hell—especially when I've already got my own thing going. The problem is that my *thing* is freelancing as a tutor online and making videos and articles to explain math concepts to kids.

I've wanted to be a math teacher since I was a teenager. Numbers just click for me. I'm pretty sure I'm the only reason Cora and Ezra passed their math classes, so I'm a decent teacher as well. But after some hands on experience in the classroom, I realized online tutoring sounded like a better option.

Still, freelancing is much different than having a steady job at a school. I think it stresses my parents out. Either that or they see it as only a college gig.

Maybe they're right.

Mom: The job is in Philly. Close to Cora.

That catches my attention. When me, Ezra, and Cora started college, we knew there might be a possibility that we'd never live in the same town again. And since Cora has been avoidant lately—*and* she's not coming home for Halloween even though she fucking promised she would—that reality seems to be setting in.

I've been secretly hoping Cora would move home after she graduated. But now I wonder if she's planning on staying in Philly. Depending on how things are with Matt at the end of the year, he may sway her decision. I hate the thought—I hate *him*—but I can't change that. No matter what, though, it's looking more and more like Cora's not going to move back home.

With a sigh, I push her from my mind. I have to finish this article, and then I have to do homework. And fuck, it's already after 8 PM.

Mom: Please just look into it. For me?

Wilder: I will. Love you.

Mom: Love you bunches, sweetie.

I smile at the old nickname. Then I pull up my browser on my laptop. If I don't do this now, I'll definitely forget. This way I can at least tell my mom I looked.

I open my personal email for the first time in weeks. I see the email from my mom, but something else catches my eye. "What the hell?" I mutter, scrolling down.

I hate email. Like, *hate* it. I never sign up for shit with my email address unless I have to, and I unsubscribe from everything the second I can. So why the fuck do I have two emails about new posts from a blog? I've never followed a blog in my damn life. But there are the subject lines, sitting right there and proving me wrong:

New Post: SELFISH

New Post: SELFISH, pt. 2

It's probably just spam, but curiosity gets the better of me anyway. Glaring at my laptop, I open the first email. I'm greeted with the only name that has the power to make my heart stop.

Cora Grimm.

"Fuck," I mutter.

Years ago—when we were in middle school—Cora started a blog. She posted the randomest shit on it. What fanfictions she was reading, who her latest celebrity crush was, some adorably bad poetry, stuff like that. She made the blog private when we were in high school. But at some point, I asked to read it again. I don't remember why.

When she gave me access, I must've given her my email address, and it must've automatically subscribed me. I just didn't know because she hasn't updated the blog in almost a decade.

Until now.

I click on the link that takes me to the post, smiling at the pink background. But my smile fades as I read what she's written.

SELFISH

Hi. Cora here. I guess I'm using this blog as a journal now. I made it private years ago, so no one can read it. And I think that's what I need right now.

I almost stop reading. If she doesn't remember she gave me access, I don't want to violate her privacy. But I can't bring myself to close the tab.

Over the past three years, she's gotten more and more distant. We still talk multiple times a week, but she doesn't open up as much. If what's in this post will help me get a better idea of what's going on in her head, I can't turn down that chance.

Groaning, I rub my face in my hands. I don't want to hurt Cora. But I need to know what's going on.

Just a couple sentences. Just read the first couple paragraphs.

"Okay," I mumble. "I can do that."

I peer at my screen.

A lot has happened since I last posted on here. Graduation, college, moving away from Wilder and Ezra (I miss them), etc. I started dating a guy named Matt. He lives with me now. It sucks. Like, my fucking god. How can a person be so stupid? So ANNOYING?

Like, today, I asked him to clean the bathroom. And he did. But he missed SO. MUCH. SHIT. The shower was still dirty. He didn't sweep. And don't get me started on the sink.

I clench my fists. Ezra and I only met Matt once, but I got bad vibes. I wrote it off as jealousy and moved on, but Cora rarely says anything good about him when we talk. She could do a lot better than him.

A couple more paragraphs. Just to see what's going on in her head.

I want to break up with him. But right now, he's my best distraction from Wilder and Ezra. I know that's stupid—why stay with a guy who makes you miserable when the only two men you've ever wanted are practically begging for your attention?

I have to reread that last sentence to make sure it says what I think it says. My mouth instantly goes dry, and I lean forward. There's no way I'm stopping now.

Matt and I aren't in love. I *know* he's not in love with me. Honestly, I'm pretty sure he's just with me because it makes for cheaper rent. Which benefits me too, but does it really? He never cleans up after himself. God, he's the fucking worst.

Last week, we were supposed to have a date night. We were just gonna stay in and watch a movie. Nothing else—we haven't had sex in, like, forever.

"Thank fuck," I mutter.

Wait. What the hell, Wilder? She's not yours.

She's not yours yet.

You know what the asshole did? He canceled! And it wasn't even like he gave me any notice. He canceled *the evening of our date*. You wanna know why? So he could hang out with his friends. Honestly, I didn't care about not getting to spend time with him. I don't really *want* to. I think we planned the date night more out of habit than anything.

But it still bugged me. I should be with someone who prioritizes me. Who I want to hang out with. Who can clean a fucking bathroom correctly. And the thing that pisses me off the most is that Matt barely gave me any notice. If he'd had the decency to cancel the day before, maybe I would've been able to hang out with Imani or Brooke or Liling.

He's selfish. So, so selfish. And it drives me nuts. But at least he's a distraction.

I don't know. I wish I could talk to Ezra or Wilder about it. But I can't. Not without explaining things I don't want to.

That's all I have for now.

XOXO, Moonflower

I smile at the last line. She's more productive and energetic at night, almost like she's nocturnal. So we nicknamed her Moonflower since they bloom after dark. *Just like she does.*

SELFISH, pt. 2 is shown as the next post at the bottom of the page, so I click on it. It was published a mere half hour after the first part.

SELFISH, pt. 2

You know what? That's not all I have for now. I have a lot more to say. A *lot,* okay?

If I'm going to call Matt selfish, then I should at least be fair and call myself selfish, too. Because I am—possibly more so than Matt.

I have a confession to make. A big, big, *big* one.

I've never been able to imagine a future with Matt. Never wanted one with him, either. I started dating him to use him to get over someone else. *Two* someone else's. My two childhood best friends.

My breath catches. *What?* Jesus fuck.

I want them both. Ezra *and* Wilder. I want to fall asleep with them both cuddling me. I want us to wake up together, a bed full of sheets and limbs and a lifelong love I'm terrified I'll never find again. I want to know what it's like to kiss them. To live with them. To have forever with them. I want their laughs and jokes and their softness and their warmth. But I want everything else, too. The raw parts of them, their rough edges, their pain and their anger.

I want it all. Every single piece of them.

And isn't that so selfish? To want both of them when I only have one of me to give? But I can't help myself. I love them both.

That's not selfish at all, Moonflower.

The reason I moved to Philadelphia wasn't because Westview has a good nursing program. That's what I told everyone, but it was a lie. I left home to put distance between myself and Wild and Ez. Being so close to them was killing me slowly. And then I started dating Matt to distract myself from them, but all it's done is make me want Wilder and Ezra *more*.

So. much. more.

I'm wrecking everything. *Everything.* And it's all because I can't stop being so fucking selfish. I just need to let them go, but I can't. I need them both.

I want Ezra's gentle kisses. I want Wilder's possessive ones. Hell, at this point, I'd take having our friendship back to the way it was. Just minus the unrequited love, please.

I dig my fingernails into my jeans. Unrequited. *Unrequited?!* If I'd known this was how she felt . . . *Shit.*

Freshman year of high school, Ezra and I both agreed neither of us would date Cora. At the time, we both had crushes on her, even though she'd been crushing on some football player.

In case that changed, we didn't want to ruin our dynamic—didn't want to make whoever didn't end up with her feel left out. And I love Cora, but I love Ezra, too. I wouldn't want to make him watch me build a life with Cora. And he couldn't stand the thought of doing the same to me, either. So we agreed that if Cora's feelings for either of us changed, we wouldn't date her. Never did we think she'd want *both* of us.

"Fuck, Moonflower," I mutter.

I've made a horrible mess of things. Not only have I pushed them away, but I can't go back. *How* am I supposed to go back home? Every time I see a picture of one of them, all I can think about are all the things I want to do to them. All the things I want them to do to me.

And trust me, there are a lot of things.

I want Wilder to chase me. I want to run away from him, and then have him catch me. And then I want him to fuck me while I pretend I don't want it. Is that weird of me? I don't know. But I think about it all the time.

I read that last paragraph again. *Holy fuck.*

I think about Ezra, too. When I came home for Christmas last year, I was hanging out at Ezra and Wilder's apartment, and I saw ropes in Ezra's room. And ever since, I've wanted him to tie me up. I want him to restrain me and then fuck my mouth until I'm choking and gagging and drooling everywhere.

There's nothing I'd like more than to surrender myself to them. For them to take away my ability to breathe, my ability to see. For them to make me feel pain in the most pleasurable ways. I want them to scare me, too. I want to be terrified of what they might do to me.

God, there's so much. But it doesn't matter. None of it matters. They're all just fantasies—ones I'll never get to live out.

I'm here, and they're back home. And it needs to *stay* that way.

Even if it hurts like hell.

XOXO, Moonflower

P.S. Wow, I can't believe I typed all of that out. Might delete it later.

I shut off my laptop and lean back in my chair, staring at the ceiling. She's been avoiding us because she's *in love* with us. It's cute, really—that she thinks she'll get away with this.

A plan forms in my mind. I'll need to get some shit, and I won't be able to tell Ezra until the last minute. He'll ask too many questions and chicken out.

Maybe it's rash, but I'm beyond caring. Cora needs us—more than she knows. And I'll destroy anything that stands between her and us.

You can't hide from us, Moonflower.

Chapter Three

Ezra

On Halloween

Wilder knocks on my bedroom door, waking me from a night of shitty sleep. Well, more like a morning and afternoon of shitty sleep.

"What?" I grunt.

Wilder opens the door, stepping inside. I blink a few times, letting my vision clear up. He's standing in the middle of my room, fully dressed and ready for the day, with his arms crossed over his chest.

"We're going to Westview. Today."

"What? Dude, that's like . . . a five hour drive."

"Do I look like I give a shit?! I'll drive. Just get out of bed and let's get moving."

"What . . ." I push myself into a sitting position as my chest tightens with panic. "Is something wrong with Cora?"

"What? No. Well, I mean, sort of. But nothing terribly urgent."

I wait for him to go on, but he doesn't. "Wild!"

"Just get dressed. It's already two o'clock. I want to be there by eight, and I'm not sure what traffic will look like."

"I need you to explain," I grouse, throwing back my covers. I stumble out of bed, throwing on the shirt Wilder hands me and then searching for some pants.

"Can't."

"Wilder *fucking* Kemp, tell me what the hell is going on!"

"Made you a sandwich. It's on the kitchen counter," he says as he starts walking out of my room. "Oh, and you should definitely shower."

"I don't need you to mother me," I snap.

He turns to me, raising an eyebrow. Doesn't have to say a single word.

"Fuck you," I grit out.

"We're leaving in a half hour."

I flip him off before storming into the bathroom.

Ever since Cora told us she wasn't coming home for Halloween, I've been in a funk. Well, that's only part of it, I suppose. Fall always has me feeling down. Something about the lack of sunlight and seasonal depression, blah blah blah. Cora tried to explain it to me once, but I wasn't in the mood to care. I love her more than I love myself, and I know she was just trying to help me. But can you help a person who has no motivation to help themself?

After quickly showering and brushing my teeth, I scarf down the sandwich Wilder made for me. It's not pleasant mixed with the lingering taste of spearmint in my mouth, but it is what it is.

Wilder comes into the kitchen from his bedroom carrying a backpack. "You'll want to pack a bag. We're spending the weekend. And we need to leave in ten minutes."

"I'm gonna kill you."

He smirks. "Oh, and pack your ropes." And then he shrugs on his black leather jacket and heads outside.

Why is he being such an asshole? And why the hell would I bring my ropes?

In my room, I shove some clothes and toiletries into a bag. I grab my sketchbook and pencils too, even though I haven't had any motivation to draw in weeks. After that, I scan my room, feeling like I'm forgetting something.

"Ready?" Wilder shouts.

With a groan, I sling my bag over my shoulder. "Coming!"

In Wilder's car, I toss my bag in the backseat. As Wilder pulls onto the road, he throws me a glance.

"Seatbelt."

"I can take care of myself," I say, pulling it on.

He doesn't answer, probably because I've been actively disproving that comment ever since I got out of bed. But what can I say? He's the one who woke me up thirty minutes ago and shoved this last-minute plan on me.

"You gonna explain?" I ask after he's pulled onto the highway.

"Do you love Cora?"

"What kind of question is that?" I spit out. "Of course I love her."

"No," Wilder says, his voice even. "I mean romantically. Sexually."

I'm silent for a long minute before I sag in my seat. I've been waiting for this moment for a long time. Gotta admit, though, I was hoping it'd never happen.

Without making it obvious, I take Wilder in. He's so . . . *put together.* His dark hair has been recently trimmed, and it's styled in a way that makes Cora stare at him for a second too long. It's not just that, though. It's everything about him. His jacket and fitted black jeans paired with his combat boots give him a sleek yet intimidating look. Or maybe it's how goddamn confident he always is.

He's perfect for Cora. Exactly what she needs.

I sigh. "Look, man. I probably should've told you this years ago. Not really sure why I didn't, honestly. But . . . If you want Cora, she's yours. I won't fight you or stand in your way."

Wilder slams on the brakes and pulls over. There's nothing in front of us, so I don't get why. Until he throws the car into park and turns to look at me. His glare is surprised. Angry, almost.

"You think I'd do that to you."

Yep. Definitely angry.

"I . . ."

"We promised we wouldn't."

"I know, but—"

"No!" he shouts. "No buts. You want to watch me marry Cora? You want to be around when we have kids? When I'm the one who's there for her more because I'd be her husband? Tell me that wouldn't be a living hell for you."

"You're good for her," I mumble.

"And so are you," Wilder snaps. "I couldn't do it, Ez. I couldn't step out of your way. Knowing she'd fall asleep in your arms every night when she could've been doing that in mine? It'd fucking gut me. And I would *never* do that to you."

Raising my hands in defeat, I say, "Okay, fine. So why the hell did you start this conversation in the first place?"

"Because maybe Cora doesn't have to choose between us. Maybe she doesn't want to choose."

"What?"

"She wants both of us, Ez."

The words hit me like a freight train. Well, not the words—the concept. *She wants me. Shit, she actually wants* me.

"Both of us." The words fall from my lips breathlessly.

He nods.

"How do you know this?"

"I can't tell you right now. Do you trust me?"

"Again, what kind of question is that?! Of course I trust you."

"Okay. Then I'm gonna tell you my plan. It won't make sense. Not remotely. But I need you to follow along with it. For Cora."

Involuntarily, my fists clench in my lap. But then I release a long breath. "Fine. For Cora. But you'd better not make me regret this."

. . .

By the time we pull up to Cora's apartment, it's dark outside. She's not here—I texted her to make sure she's already at DeAndre's and Imani's Halloween party. Matt, however, is here.

This portion of Wilder's plan makes me uneasy, but it also makes a sick part of me very happy. I've only met Matt once, but the guy gives off horrible vibes. Like, *slime* vibes. He definitely doesn't make Cora happy, so I'm not sure why she hasn't broken up with him.

Apparently, though, Wilder knows Cora wants to end things. The asshole won't reveal how, but I trust him. I just hope Cora won't be pissed at us.

Cora and Matt live in the top half of a house that's been converted into two living units. We head up the stairs quietly. About halfway up, I can't hold my tongue any longer.

"What did Matt do?" I whisper. "To make her finally decide to break up with him?"

Wilder stops right outside the door to the apartment. "How do you feel about Cora?"

"Stop being an annoying shit, Wilder. You know."

"Just answer the damn question."

I blow out a breath, the force in Wilder's eyes making me stop and actually *think*. After a minute, I grit out, "Don't make fun of me for what I'm about to say. You're acting like an asshole right now, and I don't like it."

His gaze softens. "I know. I'm sorry, I'm just pissed off. It'll all make sense soon. And I promise, I won't make fun of you." His eyes sparkle with playfulness. "Well, not about this, anyway."

I take a deep breath. Shake out my hands. "All right. Cora is . . . She's always been there, you know? With hugs or reassurances or smiles. Remember when we were trick-or-treating in fifth grade and she held my hand when I was scared to go up to that spooky house?"

Wilder smiles. "She held my hand, too. The little shit liked being scared."

"Still does, doesn't she?"

Huffing out a laugh, he nods. "You have no idea. But that's beside the point. You agree."

"With what?"

"That Cora deserves to be treasured."

I nod.

Wilder points to the door. "Matt doesn't do that. So he's done. He's fucking done, Ezra. I can't take it anymore. And she shouldn't have to, either."

"All right. Yeah, all right. Let's do this."

With that, Wilder shoves the door open. Matt is lounging on the couch watching a horror movie. When he hears us come in, he turns, a mixed expression of confusion and fear on his face.

"What the hell?" he mutters.

"Hey, buddy." Wilder gives him a nonchalant wave, which has me holding back a laugh. What angle is he playing? "We're here to help you move out."

"What?" Standing, Matt glares between the two of us. "Cora didn't tell me you guys were coming."

"Yeah, well, surprise. Pack your bags. Time to get out."

Matt laughs. "What, is this some kind of joke? It's Halloween, guys, not April Fools."

"No joke." As I say it, I come to stand next to Wilder and cross my arms over my chest. "Consider this Cora's way of breaking up with you."

Matt's jaw drops.

"Oh, and you're cleaning the bathroom before you leave," Wilder says. "It'd better be sparkling by the time you're done with it, buddy. Otherwise I'm kicking your face in."

That's . . . odd.

"Fuck you," Matt spits out. "Where the hell is Cora? She'd never do this. And stop calling me buddy."

Barking out a bitter laugh, Wilder says, "You seriously don't know where she is?" He turns to me. "Hey, Ez, why do we know where Cora is when her own boyfriend doesn't?"

"Probably because he's an idiot who doesn't know what a fucking gem he has," I reply, my glare resting steadily on Matt.

Wilder shoves him toward the bathroom. "Get to work."

"This is ridiculous! I'm not moving out. Hold on, I'm calling Cora."

When Matt pulls his phone out of his pocket, Wilder plucks it from his hand.

"Hey!" Matt exclaims.

Handing me the phone, Wilder says, "Bathroom. Now. We'll get your stuff in the car." Turning to the counter in the kitchen, he grabs a set of keys. "These are your car keys, right? They definitely aren't Cora's."

The fury on Matt's face is almost laughable. He tries to punch Wilder, but he dodges, and then I shove Matt to the ground.

"There are two of us, *buddy,*" Wilder says with a grin. "And we're both much bigger than you are. Your chances aren't looking great."

Matt may be an asshole, but at least he's not stupid. He scrambles to his feet, backing toward the bathroom door. "Fine, fine. She's more trouble than she's worth, anyway."

"You motherfucker," I growl.

Wilder grabs me and holds me back before I even realize I've started moving toward Matt. "He's the one who isn't worth it, Ez."

I let out a curse. Then I pocket Matt's phone and grab his keys from Wilder. I try them all in the front door until I find the one that works. Then I snake the key off the ring and toss it to Wilder.

"I'm gonna start getting his stuff," Wilder says. "You make sure he doesn't try anything stupid."

I nod, keeping an eye on the bathroom. It's funny, seeing Matt scrub away at the sink like he's terrified of missing a single spot.

Maybe that has something to do with why Cora is breaking up with him.

I watch as Wilder hauls a couple bags downstairs. When he comes back up, he brings a few empty boxes with him. They must've been in his trunk.

Thankfully, all the furniture and most of the stuff in the apartment is Cora's. She lived here for three years before Matt moved in with her a couple months ago.

While Wilder moves more stuff into Matt's car, I look around. A lot of the tiny apartment is the same, but there are some new additions. Mainly the black tapestry with dancing skeletons on it that's hanging above the couch. It warms my heart because it's exactly the type of thing Cora loves.

In the corner, there's a coffin bookshelf she's had since she was fifteen. Currently, there are a couple tiny jack-o-lanterns on it along with some books, a fake human skull, and some black candles.

I grin when I see the framed photo of the three of us from Halloween our senior year. It makes me happy that she still has it up, especially when I realize the photo frame is on top of her copy of *Dracula*. The three of us read it together in high school.

When Matt comes out of the bathroom, he says, "It's clean."

"I'll be the judge of that," Wilder snaps, coming out of their—*Cora's*—bedroom. In the bathroom, he inspects everything, narrowing his eyes at the mirror. "There are streaks."

"Come on man, you know how hard—"

"Again," Wilder says. "Jesus fuck. How did Cora put up with you? You should know how to clean a fucking bathroom, man."

Matt's face is beet red as he cleans the mirror again. "This is humiliating."

I hum in agreement. "I'd be ashamed of myself too if I didn't know how to look after myself."

Thankfully, Wilder doesn't give me one of his pointed looks. Because if I'm being honest, I've been a mess for the past couple months. And while I may *know* how to take care of myself, I'm not doing it. Wilder knows that better than anyone.

After Wilder approves Matt's job in the bathroom, we help him gather up the rest of his stuff. He seems resigned to his fate now, which is a relief. I want to get this over with so we can find Cora.

We watch Matt carry his last box out of the apartment and shut the door behind him. Then I turn to Wilder.

"What was up with the bathroom?"

He grins. "I'll explain soon."

Of course.

We don't leave the apartment until we watch Matt drive off. Then we make sure to lock up before we head out.

"Do you know where this party is at?"

"Yeah."

"Do I want to know how?"

"I texted Brooke. She knows we're coming."

Right. Brooke is one of the new friends Cora has made this semester. She's gotten close to a couple other girls fast. I'm happy she's finally meeting people—she struggled socially for the past three years—but it sucks, too. I hate that there are people who spend more time with her than I do.

It doesn't take long to get from Cora's apartment to the party. De-Andre and Imani's house is huge, and they went all out with their Halloween decorations. The place is the perfect blend of whimsical and creepy, with colorful lights everywhere. Jack-o-lanterns line the pathway leading up to the front door.

We park on the street. Once we're out of the car, I start to move toward the house, but then I hear Wilder opening the trunk.

"What are you doing?"

"C'mon, Ezra. We're not walking into that party without costumes."

A slow smirk spreads across my face. "What've you got?"

. . .

Inside, we're greeted with classic Halloween music and a house full of people. We scan the front room for Cora, but we don't find her. No luck in the kitchen, either.

"Wilder! Ezra! Over here."

My stomach leaps when I hear the feminine voice shouting our names over the music. But when I recognize it, I realize it's not Cora's. It's someone else's.

I turn. A young Chinese-American woman with darker skin and long black hair is looking up at me with a grin. She's flanked by two other women who're wearing similar fairy-looking costumes to hers.

"Liling, right?" I say. I've said hi to her in some of my video calls with Cora.

She nods. "And this is Imani." She gestures to her right, to a tall woman with dark brown skin and deep red locs. "And Brooke." She nods to her left, to the shortest of their group, a woman with pale skin and light brown hair.

"Right," I say. "Cora's new friends."

I'm not proud of the jealousy that slithers across my skin. But with their tiaras and makeup and happy smiles, everything clicks. Cora talks about these three all the time. And really, it's no wonder—they look like they're a blast to hang out with.

Is this why she hasn't been texting back as quickly? Because she found our replacements?

"Great to meet you," Wilder says after an awkward beat. "Do you know where Cora is?"

The three of them exchange uneasy glances, and my stomach drops through the floor.

"Is she okay?" I force out.

"Her boyfriend wouldn't stop calling her," Imani says. "She went into the library for some quiet so she could talk to him."

"Fuck," Wilder mutters. "I knew I shouldn't've given him his phone back."

Just then, a tall man with brown skin comes up behind Imani. He places a hand on her hip, eyeing us suspiciously. "Everything okay, babe?"

This must be DeAndre.

Turning her head to look up at him, Imani gives him a soft smile. "Yeah. These are Cora's best friends from home."

I grit my teeth. *Best friends from home.* Is that what Cora calls us? Not her best friends—just her best friends *from home?*

Wilder tenses next to me, and I know he's thinking the same thing.

"Ah." DeAndre grins at us. "Welcome, then. Drinks are on the counter over there. Snacks and treats are . . . well, they're kinda every-where. My wife has a sweet tooth." He kisses Imani on her temple, which makes her absolutely glow. "I'm gonna check in with Ryan and the rest of the security team. You need anything? Water?"

"I'm good. Thank you." Imani stretches upward and plants a kiss on his lips before he heads back into the party.

Liling elbows Imani. "So he's here? *He's here?*"

With a snort that Imani somehow manages to turn into something elegant, she curls an arm around Liling's waist. "I told you he's on the security team tonight. Why are you so surprised?"

"I'm not," Liling insists. "I'm just . . ."

"Nervous?" Brooke teases with a knowing smirk. "One of these days, you're going to have to actually look Ryan in the eyes. You know that, right?"

Liling lets out a flustered sound. "Whatever! Let's just dance. Or get drinks. Something!"

With a knowing chuckle, Imani pushes Liling into Brooke's arms. Then she points the way we came. "Did you see the staircase in the front room?"

We nod.

"Go upstairs. Take the hallway on the left. The library is the set of French doors on the right."

"Got it. Thank you so much," I say, dragging Wilder toward the front of the house. If Matt called Cora, we need to get to her before she starts freaking out.

"We're going to scare her," Wilder says as we climb the stairs.

"What? Scare her? That's a horrible idea."

"It's not. Trust me."

I sigh. If I hear Wilder utter those words one more time tonight, I might punch a wall. Or him. Still, I follow his lead, and we sneak into the library.

Cora's voice immediately reaches us. "Matt, what the hell are you talking about? Who's *they?* You need to be more specific." A pause. "No, I don't know! Stop being an asshole." Another pause. "You know what? I'm not dealing with your bullshit tonight."

Wilder and I creep toward her. The lights are off in here, although some light is coming through the French doors from the hallway. We stay in the shadows.

When I spot Cora, she's staring down at her phone, the light from the screen illuminating her face. The sight of her takes my breath away. Not only is her makeup immaculate, but it's . . . it's *her*. This is the first time I've seen her in person in a while.

She's barely changed at all. Her long brown hair trails down her back in loose curls. And as she always does when she's nervous, she's chewing on her bottom lip and twirling a strand of hair around one of her fingers.

It looks like she's in a similar fairy costume as the other girls, and the tiara on her head sparkles from the light from her phone. The V-neck of the dress dips low, revealing more cleavage than I'm used to her showing. The purple fabric tightens beneath her breasts before flowing loosely over her plump stomach. It stops mid-thigh, still high enough that if I bent her over, it'd show . . .

Fuck. Get it together, Ezra.

Cora is standing in between two bookshelves. It's the perfect spot for us to scare her from both sides, even though I'm half-wondering if this is a terrible idea. If she was just arguing with Matt, she's probably not in a great mood.

Still, I mirror Wilder's movements, coming around the far side of the bookshelves. We creep down the aisle quietly, the darkness concealing us for the most part. If she looked up, she'd see us. But she's frowning down at her phone still.

After a moment of hesitation, Wilder and I lock gazes. He nods, and I pull my mask down. Then we both close the distance between us, grabbing Cora at the same time.

She drops her phone and lets out a blood-curdling scream. Wilder claps a hand over her mouth as she struggles against us. Pressing her into me, he leans down and murmurs in her ear.

"Happy Halloween, Moonflower."

Chapter Four

Cora

One second, I was texting the girls to let them know I'll be down in a minute. The next, hands are grabbing me out of nowhere, I'm screaming, and the only thing I can see is Pinhead staring down at me.

As I scream, a hand is clamped over my mouth, and I realize this is it. This is how I'm going to die. If not by actual murder, then by high blood pressure and a fucking heart attack.

But then that deep, familiar voice sounds in my ear, terrifying yet comforting at the same time. "Happy Halloween, Moonflower."

Oh my god. *Oh my god.*

I let out a sob of relief. Wilder's lips brush against the shell of my ear as the tingly feeling of adrenaline rushing through my veins sets in.

Ezra pushes the Pinhead mask up, and then his hands slide around my waist. His arms encircle me, and he presses my stomach into his hips. As my eyes adjust to the dark, his smirk comes into view. "Gotcha."

If anyone else tried to scare me like this, I'd probably punch them. But my mind skips straight past anger to delight. *They're here. They came to me.*

As I throw my arms around Ezra, a giddy laugh bubbles out of me. My body is still trembling from the jump scare, but I don't care. "What the hell are you two doing here?"

"Just thought we'd surprise you," Ezra says, pressing his lips to my temple. The simple action has butterflies taking flight in my stomach even though I know it's nothing more than an innocent show of affection. "Halloween is our holiday, you know?"

I melt into him, nodding. "It is. I . . . I don't know what to say."

"How about that you're happy to see us?" Wilder tugs me from Ezra roughly, spinning me around so I'm facing him. "It's been, like, six months." He pulls me tightly against him, but not before I take in his black and red cape.

"Are you . . . are you Dracula?"

"Actually," Wilder says in a matter-of-fact tone, "Dracula was the doctor. I'm dressed as Dracula's monster."

My laugh is involuntary, even as I roll my eyes. I'd tell him it's a horrible joke, but they both know it's the type of thing I love. So instead, I bury my face into his chest, inhaling deeply. God, I've missed his smell. No, everything. I've missed *everything* about him. Both of them.

"Thank you for coming," I mumble into his costume.

I'm only able to bask in Wilder's embrace for another second before my mind ruins it. I shouldn't be surprised. I ruin everything.

Matt's angry accusations resurface. *This is how you're breaking up with me?* he asked. *Too scared to do it yourself, so you had them come kick me out. Seriously, Cora?*

Everything clicks.

Pulling away from Wilder, I glance between him and Ezra. "What did you do?"

Ezra grimaces, but Wilder grins. Nervousness has my stomach twisting in knots as I step away from both of them. My back hits the bookshelf as I realize I already know the answer to my question.

"You . . . you kicked him out of my apartment?"

"Yup." Wilder moves with me, crowding me against the shelf.

What the hell? "Why would you do that?"

"Do you love him?"

No.

"You kicked him out without knowing the answer to that?" I snap.

Wilder's grin widens. "Oh, I know it. Just want to hear you say it."

"I didn't want to break up with him."

"Don't believe you."

"I knew this was a bad idea," Ezra mutters.

"Then why did you go along with it?!" I yell, throwing my hands up in the air.

Wilder catches my wrists, pulling me into him. His fingers intertwine with mine, and he presses his lips to my knuckles while holding my gaze. It may be dark in here, but there's no mistaking what I see in his eyes.

"Wild, what—" The rest of my sentence lodges in my throat, and I can't seem to force it out.

I can't do this. Matt was my distraction. He was my excuse to not run back home and destroy what I have with Ezra and Wilder. But now . . . now they broke up with Matt *for me,* and they're here. They're fucking here. Why . . .

"Why are you here?" I whisper.

Neither of them answer. Keeping my hands in his, Wilder presses me further into the bookshelf so his body is flush with mine. His lips feather over my neck, and I gasp. This is different from how he normally touches me. This is electrifying. Sensual.

It's a struggle to keep my breaths even. He's warm and hard and unmoving, and my body reacts to him like it always has. Like the three years that I've barely seen him didn't happen. Like I can have him when I know I definitely can't.

"What are you doing?" My voice is trembling.

"Something I should've done years ago," he murmurs, leaning in.

When Wilder's lips meet mine, I melt. Like, *actually* melt. My knees give out, but he keeps me pinned to the bookshelf so I don't sink to the floor. As his mouth takes mine in a hard, demanding kiss, my thoughts turn fuzzy. He feels good. So, so good

I break our hands apart so I can grab onto his jacket. He groans into my mouth, rolling his hips into the softness of my stomach. And then he's fisting the hair at the base of my neck and forcing his tongue into my mouth.

Holy shit. I've kissed plenty of guys in my life. But never have I been kissed with such ferocity, such desperation. Such raw need. It sends chills skating across my skin in the most delicious way. My god, I never want him to stop.

But then I tense up as I remember we're not alone.

Ezra.

I pull away, shaking my head. For a painful second, my gaze locks with Ezra's. He doesn't look hurt or jealous. No, he's smiling. I don't understand why, but before I can ask, my vision blurs as tears fill my eyes.

"Moonflower," Wilder says, so gently it causes my tears to spill over. He brushes them away tenderly, kissing my cheeks as he does.

"I can't do this." I push at him, but he doesn't budge. "Wilder, let me go."

"Why?" His lips skim my jaw. There's something about his tone that makes me pause. Something dark and bitter that has all my guilt slamming into my chest at full force. "So you can run away again? Abandon us? I don't think so, Cora. We're done waiting for you to come back to us."

"But I wasn't going to come back," I whisper. *I can't.*

He chuckles lowly in my ear, pressing me harder into the bookshelf. "Funny."

"Wh . . . what?" I glance between him and Ezra, trying not to focus on Wilder's erection pressing into my stomach. "What's funny?"

"The fact that you thought we'd let you go. If you never came home, we would've dragged you back. And if we couldn't do that, then we would've chased after you until you got it through that pretty head of yours that your place is *with us.*"

He spits out the last part with such force I cringe into the bookshelf.

"Wilder," Ezra says, placing a hand on his shoulder. "You're scaring her."

"It's okay," Wilder replies with a wry smile. "She likes it. Don't you, Moonflower?"

I squirm. He's right, but I have no clue how he knows it. "What does that have to do with anything?"

"A lot," he says, his expression turning serious.

What Wilder said finally registers. *Your place is with us.* I gulp in air, but for some reason I can't get enough. My heart is racing as wildly as my thoughts, so fast I'm not sure I'll ever catch up.

"What did you mean, my place is with you?"

"Us," Wilder says firmly. "Both of us. The three of us."

I blink. Is he saying what I think he is?

Wilder.

Ezra.

Me.

. . . Together?

"What?" I choke out.

Patiently, they wait for me to process, Wilder stroking his fingers up and down my bare arm. Ezra watches me uneasily, and my eyes lock with his in a stare that absolutely guts me.

"Cora," Ezra murmurs.

I want to go to him, but I'm frozen in place.

They kicked Matt out.

Broke up with him for me.

Then they came here.

And Wilder . . . kissed me

"You both want me." I hear the words before I realize I've spoken them.

Fear flickers over Ezra's expression, but he nods.

I shake my head, disbelief setting in. There's no way. No fucking way. It was a selfish fantasy. One that I should've put to bed years ago.

"But—"

Wilder clamps a hand over my mouth. "If you're about to say something about how it's selfish of you, don't you fucking dare."

When he moves his hand, I start again. "But it is."

"Cora," he growls.

I bite my tongue.

"This is happening, Moonflower." Wilder tips my chin up with a single finger. "We've waited long enough."

Long enough.

I don't have time to think about the implication behind what he said before Wilder slams his lips to mine again. Both his hands hold my head, twisting into my soft curls. But then he curses, breaking off the kiss before I want him to.

He spins me around and shoves me toward Ezra. Almost instantly, Ezra's arms encircle me. That fear is back in his eyes, and I think I know why, but I can't find it in me to say what he needs to hear.

"Ez," I whisper, grabbing onto his black hoodie.

"I know," he says, his voice soothingly calm as he holds me close. And then he kisses me, softly and slowly, just how I always imagined he would.

What I don't expect, though, is for him to pick me up and spin me around before setting me on the floor again. I squeak in surprise, but it's a *pleasant* surprise.

Ezra smiles against my mouth before pulling away the tiniest bit. "This okay?"

"Yes. More, Ez. Please."

That's all it takes for him to kiss me again, this time in a deeper, harder way. It's similar to how Wilder kissed me yet somehow different. Ezra's lips move against mine firmly but not demandingly. He tastes almost sweet, and I tentatively run my tongue across his bottom lip. When his lips part, I slip inside.

His tongue dances with mine, a series of gentle caresses and licks. Then he pulls away, giving me one last small kiss when I whine in disappointment. "I need you to say it, Moonflower."

"It's not fair to you," I whisper. "Either of you."

"That's for us to decide. And you know how we feel. So just say it, Cora."

I can't look away from him. Ezra has captured my gaze completely, just like he and Wilder have done with my heart. So I swallow my worries and my doubts. And then, even though I'm terrified that they'll be too much or I won't be enough, I say it.

"I want both of you."

Ezra's face lights up like he's found a treasure chest, and I wonder if that's what I am to him—a treasure. He presses another kiss to my mouth before I feel Wilder come up behind me and rest his hands on my hips.

Nervousness—and something far more pleasurable—curls in my belly. "What . . . What happens now?"

"I think you know the answer to that, Moonflower," Ezra replies.

I definitely have ideas. And hopes, and dreams, and probably five different fantasies about how things could unfold in the next minutes . . . or hours.

Wilder places a kiss to my shoulder. Then a few up my neck and my soft jawline. "Your heart rate just picked up, pretty girl. Are you nervous? Or excited?"

"Both," I whisper. "Definitely both."

Ezra captures my mouth in a slow, heated kiss, gripping my chin in between his fingers. "You can tell us to stop."

"I don't want you to."

He smirks. "Good."

And then Ezra is holding my face and kissing me again, and Wilder's hands are traveling over my stomach, working their way downward. He pulls the skirt of my dress up, and I whimper when his fingers slide into my underwear.

"Wild," I groan into Ezra's mouth when he finds my clit.

"You're soaked, Moonflower. Is this because we scared you?"

"Because of . . ." I gasp when Wilder pinches my clit gently. "Because of everything. Because of you. Both of you."

"Fuck," Wilder mutters, circling my clit gently.

I've never done anything sexual with more than one person at a time before. Having Ezra kiss me while Wilder fingers me is new and different. Overwhelming, but in the best way. Still, I'm not sure who to focus on—Ezra as his lips move against mine, or Wilder while he works me toward an orgasm.

Eventually, Ezra pulls away, making up my mind for me. Then he tugs down the straps of my dress, and I thread my arms through them so he can pull the fabric down. I expect to feel a wave of insecurity, but I don't. I love my body—every soft, supple, thick part of me—and Wilder and Ezra have always adored me for who I am.

"Shit." With a groan, Ezra leans down and buries his face in between my bare breasts, squeezing them with his hands. He pinches my nipples gently. "Cora. So fucking beautiful."

Before I can reply, Ezra sucks one of my nipples into his mouth. It wrenches a moan from me, and I have to fight to stay standing.

I love having them touch me, but it's not enough. I need to touch them, too. So I palm Ezra's dick through his jeans, gasping when I realize how big he is. *Oh god.* It's hard to touch Wilder since he's behind me, but I manage to reach my other hand behind me and thread my fingers through his hair.

Swearing under his breath, Ezra grinds into my hand. "Make her come, Wild. I need to be inside her."

"I get her first," Wilder growls.

Ezra rolls his eyes as he huffs out a laugh. "I know."

"What should I do to you, Cora?" Wilder murmurs in my ear. "Should I fuck you against this bookshelf? Make you come with my mouth and then my dick? Or should I use you up like the pretty plaything you are?"

I don't have a chance to respond before his filthy words cause my orgasm to slam into me. He clamps his free hand over my mouth as I cry out. Then he shoves his fingers into me, curling them just so and adding another wave of pleasure.

All of it. All of it and so much more.

Wilder slowly pulls his fingers out of me before shoving them into my mouth. "Suck."

Ezra watches with fire in his eyes as I suck my salty taste from Wilder's fingers. Then, once I'm done, Ezra fuses his mouth to mine. His tongue plunges into my mouth, chasing after the lingering taste of my arousal. When he's done, we both gasp for air, and I find my fingers tightening around his cock.

Wilder turns me so I'm facing him. After an appreciative glance at my breasts, he says, "I'm going to fuck this pretty mouth of yours, and you're going to take every drop of my cum down your throat like a good girl. And then Ezra is going to have you whatever way he wants. Understood?"

My nod is involuntary, almost like I'm in a trance.

Yes. Yes, yes, yes.

"Get on your knees, Moonflower."

I do, and Wilder leans over me, placing a hand on the shelf above my head. Then he grips my jaw with his other one, forcing it open.

"Tongue out."

I obey.

He spits in my mouth, and my god, I never thought I'd like someone doing that. But now I want him to do it again, so I stretch upward with a little moan, making him smirk.

"You want more?"

I nod.

He spits on my tongue, gazing down at me with a fiery, dark, lustful gleam in his light brown eyes. "Swallow, pretty girl."

Holding his gaze, I do as he says. And then I open my mouth again, showing him I'm ready. That I want him.

As Wilder undoes his belt, he says, "All you have to do is tap my thigh, and I'll stop."

My eyes widen when he pulls out his cock. It looks as big as Ezra's. Maybe *too* big for this.

"You can handle it, Cora. I want to feel you choke around my dick while you struggle to take me down your throat."

I whimper, opening my mouth wider and tilting my head back for him. Gently, he pushes a few strands of hair out of my face. Then he smears a bead of precum over my bottom lip. I can't help myself—I dart my tongue out to taste him.

"Fuck," he whispers.

He pauses and stares at me, his cock not even a half-inch from my lips. Maybe this is what's doing it for him—what's making this feel real for him. Because he's gazing down at me with so many emotions on his face that for a second, I think he might cry.

Gently, I place a hand on his thigh. "Wild?"

"I love you. You're about to feel like I fucking hate you, but I don't. I love you more than the moon and the stars, Cora."

"I know," I whisper, squeezing his leg. "I love you, too."

He still seems frozen. Like he's fantasized about this moment for years, just like I have. It's a lot to handle, especially from his perspective. I've done my best to keep him and Ezra at arms' length for three years. And now I'm here, on my knees in front of him, like he hasn't been hurting inside this whole time. Everything's been flipped upside down in a matter of hours.

I don't know what to say—don't think there's anything I can say. So instead, I take the tip of his cock into my mouth and suck lightly.

"Cora," he chokes out. His hand tightens in my hair, and I can only imagine how hard he's gripping the shelf. "Do that again."

I do, watching as his eyes slide closed. He swears under his breath, pumping his hips forward.

The second he hits the back of my throat, I gag. He groans, pulling out and thrusting in again, eliciting the same reaction. Then he keeps his strokes shallow, letting me adjust while I blink back my tears.

"Have you had anyone do this before? Fuck your pretty throat?"

I nod as much as I can.

"Anyone this big?"

I shake my head.

"Okay." He strokes my jawline. "I'll try to be gentle."

Another shake of my head, and he raises an eyebrow. I can just barely make out his satisfied, knowing smirk.

"Our girl likes it rough, Ez. Well, if that's what you want, Moonflower . . ." Wilder grabs my hair, wrapping it around his hands. And then he yanks me forward, shoving his hips into me at the same time. "Shit," he grunts when I gag again.

I try to relax my throat. Really, I do. But I just end up choking again, making my tears finally overflow. For a moment I worry about my make-up, but Wilder's fingers tightening in my hair pull me back to the present.

"Too much?" he asks. I expected him to say it teasingly, but he sounds more concerned than anything.

"No, I can take it. Just . . . a little slower at first, maybe."

"Of course," he murmurs.

This time, I'm able to take him down without as much trouble. Wilder slides all the way into my throat with a shudder. I know I won't be able to breathe, but I try anyway, and it makes me choke. Wilder holds my head still as he pumps into me a few times.

"Cora. Cora, fuck."

I can tell he doesn't want to, but he pulls out. It gives me the chance to gulp in air, even though I'd prefer he didn't give me the option.

"Don't stop, Wild. I'll let you know when I need a break."

He runs the tip of his cock over my lips. And then, after I've taken another breath, I open my mouth wide. He lets me take him down my throat at my own pace, but he loses his self-control after that.

"You feel so goddamn good," he grits out. As he fucks my throat with relentless strokes, he uses my hair to hold my head still. His grip is so tight it brings more tears to my eyes.

Wilder wasn't kidding when he said it'd feel like he doesn't love me. This . . . the way he's pumping into me—using me—feels heartless. Degrading, like I'm nothing more than a toy. *His plaything.* And god do I love it.

Knowing Ezra is watching makes it even better. I can feel his heated gaze on me, slithering down my body. I want him to touch me too, but I also want to focus solely on them one at a time. Wilder might get me first, but that doesn't mean I'm any less excited to be with Ezra.

I'm gripping Wilder's jeans so hard they start to slide down his legs. My mind is caught between chanting *just a little longer, just a little longer, just a little longer,* and trying to enjoy the feeling of being so thoroughly and brutally used.

I used to fuck my throat with a dildo and pretend it was either Wilder or Ezra. To be perfectly honest, I did it yesterday with my head hanging off the edge of my bed and my free hand working furiously in between my legs.

This, though? This is the real thing, and I never want Wilder to stop.

My throat has different ideas, though. And after a minute, I find myself tapping on Wilder's thigh. He doesn't protest or try to keep going. One second my throat is bulging and full, and the next it's empty. As I cough and gasp in breaths, he re-wraps my hair around his hands. He keeps his hold tight, like he can't bear the thought of letting go of me.

Once I've caught my breath, Wilder bends at his waist and kisses me gently, a complete one-eighty from what he just did. "You're doing so well, pretty girl," he mutters against my lips. "And your throat is so fucking tight." Another kiss.

"More?" I whisper.

"Oh, definitely."

With that, he enters my mouth again. I can feel how wet and warm my panties are, and as Wilder takes away my ability to breathe again, I wonder if he and Ezra can smell how turned on I am.

"Keep your throat relaxed, Moonflower. You can do it."

I hum, partially for him and partially to distract my gag reflex as he shoves into my throat.

Wilder groans. "Such a good girl."

From there, it's all I can do to hold onto his legs. Tears stream from my eyes, drool drips from my chin, and eventually I can't help but gag.

"I'm gonna come, Cora. Christ, shit, *fuck.*" Wilder throws his head back, pulling out enough that his cum coats my tongue and some hits the back of my throat.

I swallow it all like he told me to, savoring the taste. Then I suck gently on his tip before releasing him from my mouth.

"Fuck," he groans. I don't think I've ever heard him so breathless before. When he falls to his knees in front of me, he devours my mouth. His hands leave my hair and wrap around my throat, not squeezing, just holding.

"I love you," I say against his lips, relishing in how he eats up the words.

He nips at my bottom lip. "You're mine, you hear me? Mine, Cora."

For the first time since I got on my knees, I glance at Ezra. I know what his problems are, and there's no way I'm going to make them worse. I could never. So when I breathe out the word, "Yours," it's his dark eyes I'm staring into, not Wilder's.

Ezra is leaning against the bookshelf, his hands shoved into the pockets of his jeans. When Wilder releases me, I don't wait for Ezra to tell me what to do. I just get onto my hands and knees and crawl to him, maintaining eye contact the whole time. It feels right, so I don't question it.

When I'm in front of him, I smile up at him. I can only make out some of his features in the dark, but he looks handsome nonetheless.

"Get up here."

I scramble to my feet. My hands go to his chest, splaying over his hard muscles. Our mouths meet like two oceans colliding, powerful waves crashing against each other endlessly.

"Shit, Moonflower. What I'd do to make that mouth of yours taste like me."

"I wouldn't stop you," I whisper.

But he shakes his head. "Not tonight. I have other plans for you."

I shiver in anticipation.

Ezra turns me around so I'm facing the shelf. His hand skims down my back before squeezing my ass. "Bend over, Cora."

I'm not used to him being so commanding, but I kind of like it. So I obey, even though I know I'm exposing myself by doing so. When he traces a finger down the center of my panties, I whimper.

"Grab onto the bookshelf."

I do, moaning when he kneels and pulls my underwear down my legs. Then I lean into the bookcase as I step out of them.

"Spread your legs, Moonflower." Ezra runs his hands up my thighs, caressing my stretch marks before kissing them.

I don't dare disobey. Not when I'm so close to getting everything I've ever wanted.

I can feel Ezra's gaze on me—feel his breath against my skin. It's almost like a form of torture—having his mouth so close but not on me. I want to push myself into his face, but I don't. We've been pining after each other for years. If he needs a minute, just like Wilder did, I can give it to him.

"Fuck," I hear Ezra whisper. Then his tongue parts me, and he groans, so deeply and wantonly I'm almost surprised.

But it's not a surprise, not really, because I feel the same way.

Ezra's tongue finds my clit, flicking it gently, then circling it. As I grip the bookshelf harder, I realize my mouth won't taste like him, but *his* mouth will taste like *me*. And oh my god, why do I love that so much?

I want to kiss him when he's done.

Gripping my ass cheeks, Ezra plunges his tongue into me. I'm not sure a man has ever eaten me out with so much enthusiasm. It's like he's trying to get drunk off of me, like he needs more, more, *more*.

When he sucks my clit into his mouth, I yelp.

"Oh my god. *Ohmygod*, Ezra."

He replies with a low hum, too focused to stop.

Something warm and wet drips onto my thigh, and for a moment I wonder if I'm *too* turned on. If it's silly, how badly I've wanted them for most of our friendship. But then Ezra finally pulls away, just for a second.

"I fell asleep to the thought of doing this to you for years, Moonflower."

He dives back in, wrenching a half-sob, half-cry from somewhere deep inside of me. His words soothe my anxious thoughts, pushing them out of my head and bringing me back to him.

After a minute, Ezra slips a single finger into me. It's simultaneously too much and not enough, and I can't help but push back into him. He chuckles as he hits one of my sensitive spots, and all of a sudden it's definitely, one hundred percent *not enough*.

"Ezra," I groan. "Please."

He stands, and I hear the sound of him undoing his belt. "I can't wait any longer."

The next thing I know, he's slamming into me. He doesn't give me a chance to adjust, but I've been so turned on for so long I don't need to.

"Christ," he wheezes.

I whimper as he thrusts into me repeatedly. The feeling of being filled to the brim, of him hitting all the right spots, makes it ridiculously hard to keep standing. But I manage, pushing back every time he thrusts forward, taking him deeper.

"I want to kiss you," I beg.

He yanks me up, holding me so my back is pressed into him. Grabbing my chin, he turns my head so he can capture my mouth in a heated, possessive kiss. I was right—he tastes like me. It satisfies something deep inside of me that I didn't know existed until this moment.

Why I expected Ezra to be sweet and gentle is beyond me. Don't get me wrong—this is a thousand times better. It's just not how he normally acts.

"Play with your clit, Cora. I need to feel you come." His hand that was gripping my chin slides down over my throat, squeezing the sides just enough that I moan.

One of my hands snakes in between my legs, and I rub my clit the way I like.

"God, I love how obedient you are," Ezra whispers before nibbling on the shell of my ear.

I groan, moving my fingers faster. They slip, going too far, and I brush against Ezra's cock as it moves in and out of me. I let my fingers stay there for a moment, trying to cement in my head just how real this is. Then I move back to my clit.

"Shit." Ezra grabs my chin and turns me to him again. As his lips move against mine, he continues thrusting into me, and the new angle is like experiencing heaven on earth. "Fuck, Cora. I'm gonna come. I need to come inside you."

"Yes," I cry. "Please, Ezra."

His grip on me tightens. And then he groans, his hips slowing. "Oh god, oh god, oh my god, Cora."

I think it's because I've thought about it so many times. Wanted it so badly for so many years. Because when he comes, I do, too, in the most explosive, mind-numbing way.

Thankfully, the bookshelf is in reach, because my orgasm hits me with dizzying force. I grab onto it, moving my finger lightly over my clit as Ezra finishes inside of me.

As we both come down, he holds me close to him. We're both shaking, and my mind is absolutely racing.

Holy shit.

Holy fucking shit.

Did all that actually happen?

"Cora. You're still on birth control, right?" There's a hint of worry in Ezra's voice.

"I am, yeah."

"Thank fuck," he mutters, pressing his forehead to my shoulder. Then he straightens, taking the straps of my costume and helping me back into them.

"Where did my underwear go?" I ask, searching the floor for them.

"I've got them here," Wilder says, holding them above my head when I reach for them.

"Wild! I need those."

He pulls a pair of folded-up, orange panties from his pocket and hands them to me. "Grabbed these from your drawer. Was always planning on keeping the ones you wore tonight."

Ezra snickers. "You're fucking obsessed."

"What, like you're not?"

Ezra grins, grabbing my face and kissing me. "Definitely am."

"I . . . uh, I'm gonna clean up in the bathroom," I say, snatching the orange panties from Wilder. "Deal with my makeup and . . . everything."

"Awww," Wilder coos. "She's too embarrassed to say that she's soaked for us. Or that she has your cum dripping out of her, Ezra."

"Shut up," I mutter, brushing past them both.

But Wilder grabs my arm and pulls me back, pinning me to his chest. "I will never stop talking about the fact that you're ours. *Never.*"

He slams his lips to mine, gripping my sides like he's trying to leave marks. When he releases me, he grins down at me. And even though I'm blushing harder than I ever have, I can't help but smile back.

Ezra comes up behind me, pressing a kiss to my shoulder. "You're ours now, Moonflower. That's never changing."

This time, I hold Wilder's gaze. "Yours. Forever."

Chapter Five

Wilder

When Cora comes out of the bathroom, I can't help but snicker. She's cleaned up her makeup and straightened her tiara, but she doesn't look nearly as pristine as she did when we found her.

She narrows her eyes at me. "What?"

I shrug.

"Wild!"

"It just looks like . . . well, either like you got absolutely ravaged by your two best friends or you had one hell of a crying session."

A slow grin creeps over her face. "It was kinda both."

With a laugh, I take her into my arms and kiss her. Now that we have her, I can't seem to stop touching her.

When we break off our kiss, my Cora's eyes are sparkling. "This changes everything, doesn't it?"

"Yeah," I say softly.

Just like that, her eyes fill with tears. "I'm so stupid," she whispers. "Oh my god, I had everything wrong. Guys, I'm sorry." Her voice breaks on the last word, and she covers her mouth with her hand.

"Hey," Ezra says, pulling her into his arms gently. "Cora, what's wrong?"

"I pushed you away," she sobs. "I wanted you both so badly, but I never thought this would happen, so I just . . ." She shakes her head before leaning her forehead against his chest. "I'm sorry. I didn't want to hurt you guys. But every time I looked at you, every time I was around you, it was so *painful.*"

Realization settles on Ezra's features. He kisses the top of her head, staring at me, probably expecting me to have a shocked expression similar to his. But I already know all this. I've known for a couple weeks.

"I didn't know you felt that way," Ezra murmurs. "I never thought you'd want . . . both of us."

"Of course I do," she says, pulling away so she can look at him. "Of *course* I want you both. Ez, how could I not?" Her fingers brush across his cheek while she stares up at him through teary eyes.

Ezra doesn't know what to say to that, so he just watches her. Then he sighs, wiping away her tears as they fall. "I dunno."

"I'm so sorry," she whispers, turning to look at me too. "I shouldn't've done it. Even though it was hard to be around you two, I still should've prioritized you both. Anything else wasn't fair to you guys, and I missed you so much."

I'm not really sure what to say. I've been a mix of angry, confused, and hurt for years. Reading her blog posts helped clear a lot of things up, but all her avoidance feels like it was for nothing now. If this was going to be the end result, maybe we would've gotten here sooner if she hadn't pushed us away.

Or maybe we all would've suffered in silence for the rest of our lives.

Maybe it's stupid, but most of me doesn't care. I just want her. I want the three of us together again. And I'm pretty sure that's what they want too.

Stepping up to them, I put one arm around Ezra and one around Cora. "I get it, Moonflower. I wish you would've said something, but I understand why you didn't. You were scared."

She sniffles, staring at me in baffled silence.

"I'll probably have questions at some point," Ezra says. "But the important thing is that all that shit is behind us. I'm not wasting the time I have with you by letting old wounds fester. We'll have to rebuild some, sure. But let's focus on *that*. Not the past. Okay?"

She nods. "Okay."

Cora tries to smile, but she's still crying. It breaks my heart because I know this has been hard on her, too. She had a horrible choice to make, and both options resulted in pain. Maybe things could've been different if she'd said something earlier, but honestly, I'm not sure if I would've been willing to share Cora a few years ago. I've grown up a lot in the past couple years.

"Hey." Ezra pulls his mask over his face. Then, in what I'd categorize as a horrible Pinhead voice, he says, *"No tears, please. It's a waste of good suffering."*

Cora lets out a tearful laugh, shoving him playfully. "You're a fucking dork, you know that?"

"Yeah. But I'm your dork. Aaaaand you love me."

Her expression softens, and for a moment I'm worried she's going to start crying all over again. She doesn't, though—just nods and says, "A lot."

After that, her tears dry up. She has to fix her makeup again, but Ezra and I don't mind waiting. Once she's come out of the bathroom, I take her hand in mine, and she grabs Ezra's. We walk downstairs like that, the three of us refusing to let go of each other. Pinhead, a fairy, and Dracula. I can only imagine it's one hell of a sight.

All I want to do is take Cora back to her apartment and continue what we started in the library, but she seemed excited about this party. I may not leave her side all night, but I'm not going to take her away from her friends, either. Besides, I'm sure her body needs some type of break.

The past three years of agonizing distance still hurt, but after reading her blog posts last week, everything makes more sense. And it couldn't be more clear that Cora was hurting, too. She must've been so lonely.

Downstairs, we run into Liling, Imani, and Brooke almost immediately. They're in one of the larger rooms swaying to the music, red cups in their hands.

When Brooke spots us, she squeals, grabbing onto Cora and pulling her over. "Where have you been?! We've been waiting for you."

"I was . . ." Cora straightens her fairy costume. "Busy."

I'm barely able to hide my smile by asking, "You want something to drink, Cora?"

She nods.

"I'll get it," Ezra says. "You want anything, Wild?"

I shake my head. One of us needs to stay sober tonight, and it makes sense that it should be me since I drove.

Ezra goes to get drinks, and the girls immediately start chattering about this Ryan guy. Liling looks especially flustered.

"You both *obviously* like each other," Cora says. "Why haven't you done anything about it?"

Liling gulps down half of the liquid in her cup before saying, "He's older than I am! What if it doesn't work out? What if he wants kids? Because I don't think I do. And what if—"

"LILING."

She groans, smacking her palm to her forehead. "Am I overthinking things again?"

"Babe," Imani says. "It's what you do best."

"Just give it a try," Brooke says, throwing an arm haphazardly around Liling's shoulders. Some of the liquid from her cup spills onto the wooden floor. "It could end up being the best thing that ever happened to you."

Cora gives Brooke a concerned look. "How many drinks have you had?"

A large man with long, dark blond hair comes up behind Brooke. "I've got her, don't worry."

"Oh, hi Blaze."

He gives Cora a tight smile before tucking Brooke into his side. She giggles, nestling into him with a happy sigh. Once upon a time, seeing a couple as head-over-heels in love as they obviously are would've made me jealous. But not anymore.

Fuck, that's a good feeling.

Ezra comes up next to me and hands Cora one of the drinks in his hands.

Blaze casts a suspicious glance over me and Ezra. "Friends of yours, Cora?"

"Yeah! Um. My . . . boyfriends."

Goddamn, that's an even better feeling.

Brooke's eyes bug out of her head. "WHAAAAT? You told me they were just your friends! Wait. Waitwaitwait. What happened to Matt?"

Cora takes Brooke's questions in stride. "I'll tell you when you're sober, hon. I don't think you'd remember anything right now."

With a groan, Brooke leans into Blaze. "I'm not drunk. I promise."

Blaze chuckles. "Yeah you are, you dork."

Imani looks over me, Ezra, and Cora with a knowing smirk. "Can't wait to hear all the *details.*"

Cora blushes so deeply, Ezra chuckles when he sees it. Then he kisses her on the cheek. "Have fun, babe."

The second Ezra starts pulling me away, Cora's face falls and panic fills her eyes. "You aren't leaving, are you?"

She's joking, right?

Oh shit, she looks like she's gonna cry.

"We're here all weekend," Ezra assures her. "I just don't want to take you away from your friends too much."

She relaxes instantly. "Okay. Thank you. You won't go too far?"

"Definitely not," I say, planting a firm kiss on her lips. "Now go spend time with them because you're ours for the next two days."

With a radiant smile, she turns back to the girls, who look like they have a hundred questions each. Ezra and I retreat to the corner of the room and watch her.

I hope things will be different from here on out.

Of course, I know they will be. But I want *everything* to change. I want Cora to go back to telling us every little thought that goes through her head. I want Ezra to get some fucking help. See a therapist or get on antidepressants or something. And I want . . . well, I want the three of us to spend the rest of our days together doing whatever the fuck makes us happy.

My phone buzzes in my pocket, and I pull it out.

Mom: Did you ever look at that job listing?

With a sigh, I show the text to Ezra. I told him about what she sent me last week and may have gone on a slight rant. He listened to the whole thing without a peep. That's Ezra for you. He's always been good at that.

"The shit you do pays your bills," Ezra says. "Don't know why she doesn't get that."

"It's steady work, too," I reply. "I think she's just scared because it's all online."

Ezra gives me a knowing look. Hell, he has it harder than I do. Imagine having parents who're supportive of you pursuing an art career. Don't think that's happened in the history of ever. But he's making it work somehow. Putting his work on print-on-demand sites, taking commissions online, shit like that.

"Maybe if you showed her proof," Ezra suggests. "That's what got my parents on board. I showed them how I was actually making money, practically shoved the bank transactions in their faces. It made it make a little more sense to them. And you, you can show them all those comments you get from kids who're thanking you for helping them."

"Yeah," I mumble, staring at my phone. "Maybe I'll try that."

The thing is, I can't help but wonder if my mom is right. What happens if this site decides they don't need me anymore? Or if I mess it up somehow? My school workload is already heavy enough this semester. What if I can't keep up with deadlines—with homework or this job?

Plus, freelancing is already risky. It comes with more freedom, but it can trap you, too. I'm not an employee, so I don't get benefits. No health insurance, no paid time off, no sick days, none of that shit. Honestly, thinking about that is stressful as hell.

And now—not that it's a bad thing—we finally have Cora. We'll be five hours away for the rest of the school year, which is going to hurt like hell. There's no way Ezra and I aren't going to make it out to Philly more often. Or maybe we can meet her somewhere halfway. Regardless, it's going to mean less free time for working.

Sagging into the corner, I sigh. It'll be worth it. I wouldn't trade a second of the time I have with Ezra and Cora for the world. But these coming months are going to be really fucking stressful.

Ezra nudges me gently. "Stop."

"What?"

"Stop worrying. Just be here. With her. With us."

When I look at him, I'm equally surprised and relieved to see that his smile reaches his eyes. *Fuck.* I can't think of the last time I've seen that.

Cora isn't some magic cure. There's no way Ezra's depression is just going to vanish because we're together now. But if it helps even a little bit, that's a huge weight off my shoulders. I've tried to help him, but there's only so much I can do. And I'm not the most patient person either.

After a while, Cora catches my gaze from across the room. She meanders over to us, a sleepy smile on her face. The party is winding down, and Brooke and Blaze already left. At this point, I'm ready to get her out of here.

Once she's next to us, Cora yawns, leaning her head against Ezra's chest.

He kisses the top of her head. "Time to go home, Moonflower?"

She nods, snaking her arms around Ezra's waist. He laughs, peeling her off of him before clasping her hand in his.

We say goodbye to Cora's friends, and then we head to my car. Ezra helps Cora into the passenger seat and buckles her in before slipping into the back. After I start driving, Cora tentatively places her hand on my thigh. It's a foreign feeling, even though I've wanted her to do it every time I've driven her somewhere.

I cover her hand with mine, keeping my other hand on the steering wheel. We still have all of tomorrow and at least half of Sunday with her, but it already feels like it's going by too fast. There's no way I'm not savoring every second, every glance, every touch.

Especially since things might go south from here. At some point, I have to admit that I read Cora's blog posts. I know Ezra will be mad I didn't tell him everything from the start. And Cora—she wrote those posts thinking no one would read them. It was a violation of her privacy that I did.

Can't find it in me to regret it, though. We're all much better off now.

Once we're inside Cora's apartment, I sigh. The longer I wait, the worse this is gonna be. Thankfully, she gives me an excuse to wait, though.

"I'm gonna shower," she says, looking down at herself. "And get out of this sweaty costume."

I breathe a sigh of relief as she heads into the bathroom. My reprieve is only temporary, though, because Ezra is giving me a hard look.

"She's gonna have questions."

"I know."

"*I* have questions."

"Yeah, Ez, I know." I rub my face. How the hell am I supposed to confess without blowing everything up? Man, I really didn't think this through.

When Cora comes out of the shower, she's beaming. She changed into sweatpants and an old T-shirt—her usual attire—and it makes me happy, seeing her this way. Relaxed and not worried that she has to perform in front of us.

First, she kisses Ezra, twisting her fingers into his hoodie. Then she kisses me, her eyes glowing with a happiness that makes me hate myself for what I'm about to do.

Just get it over with. Don't draw this out.

"I have a confession to make," I say tightly.

She tenses in my arms. "What?"

"I read your blog."

Cora's face falls, and she takes a step back from me. "You . . . you did *what?*"

Chapter Six

Ezra

"I read your blog," Wilder says again, holding her gaze.

"Her blog?" I ask. "What does that have to do with anything? It hasn't been updated in years."

"Until a couple weeks ago," Wilder corrects. He's still staring at Cora, who's gone from ghostly pale to beet red in a matter of seconds.

Gently, I pull her to one of the chairs at the little table in the kitchen. She plops onto it, blinking confusedly.

"But . . . how?" she says.

"You gave me access after you made it private. I don't remember why or when exactly. It was some time in high school."

Cora narrows her eyes. "Yeah, I think I remember that. But Wild, those were private. Why did you read them?"

"Why do you think?"

"Don't play games, Wild," I snap. My hand is resting on Cora's shoulder, and I give her a reassuring squeeze. "That wasn't fair and you know it."

I don't want to gang up on him, but what the fuck? He'd better have one hell of an explanation.

"Those were private entries," she says softly.

He doesn't say anything, so I shoot him a glare.

With a sigh, Wilder moves toward Cora. He kneels in front of her, taking her hands in his. "I'll admit that it was wrong. I didn't want to break your trust, Moonflower, and I'm sorry I did. But I'm not sorry for where it got us. Not one bit."

I can tell from her voice that she's holding back more tears. Still, she manages to ask, "Why did you read them?"

For a second, he stares at their hands, clasped together in her lap. Then he looks up into her eyes. "To be honest? I fucking missed you. Reading the entries helped me understand why you held us at arm's length. But before I read them? Fuck, Cora, I had no clue what was going on."

She sags into her chair. "I'm sorry."

"Hey," I say, crouching down next to Wilder. "You already apologized. You never have to do it again, okay?"

She nods, giving me a weak and unconvincing smile.

Wilder continues, "I read your blog because I was worried about you. Trust me, I know it doesn't justify what I did. But I didn't know what else to do. It's been three years of missing you and wondering what the hell went wrong. And I can't lie, Moonflower, it's been painful."

"I know," she whispers.

"I know you do," he murmurs, kissing her knuckles. "It hurt you, too."

She nods. "A lot."

"And that's why I read the entries," he says. "I was worried, I missed you, I love you, and I needed to understand what was going on in that head of yours. Should I have kept reading? Probably not. But once I saw the part about how you felt about me and Ez, there's no way I could've stopped, Cora. Not if there was a chance we could make this work."

"So that's how you knew," I say, turning to look at him. "That's how you knew she wanted both of us. And how you knew what she'd like."

He nods.

Cora is silent, staring at her and Wilder's hands. Every second of quiet has me getting more and more anxious. Fuck, if this is over before it starts—

"Would you do it again?" she asks.

"Yes."

"Wilder!" I exclaim.

He looks into Cora's eyes and says, "If you pushed us away again, without a doubt, yes. I'd do it in a fucking heartbeat. I'm not letting you go again, and I'll do whatever it takes to keep you. *Whatever* it takes."

Thankfully, Cora doesn't shy away from his words. She's used to his possessiveness by now. "I guess the lesson here is that I shouldn't hide things from you guys," she mumbles.

Squeezing her hands, Wilder says, "I'm not going to go behind your back unless I have good reason to. I just didn't know how else to make sure you were okay. You weren't telling us anything."

"I know. I'm sorry."

I shake my head. "You don't have to apologize again."

With a tired laugh, she says, "Oh, you'll probably hear it plenty over the next couple days."

Her words make me sigh. She's always had a complex about having to make up for herself. Cora has never seen herself as enough, and she's constantly apologizing for herself and every little mistake she makes.

You don't have to do that with us, Moonflower.

"I should probably let you read the entries, too," Cora says to me.

"Only if you want."

"I think it'd be a good idea. Not tonight, though."

My hand trails across her shoulders. "Of course. You tired?"

She nods. "Exhausted."

With a quick glance to Wilder, I ask, "Are we good? The three of us?"

"I'm good if you're good," Wilder replies.

Cora nods, looking at me questioningly.

Am I pissed at Wilder? Some, yeah. He could've told me everything on the drive here. But if I'm being honest, I'm glad he didn't. I don't think I would've had the guts to follow through with his plan if I'd known about her secret confession. So I smile at them both.

"I'm good."

"You guys are sleeping in my bed, right?"

"Nonnegotiable," Wilder says, kissing her lightly.

In Cora's room, she groans. "We should change the sheets."

"I got them earlier." Wilder nudges her toward the bed. "Don't worry about it."

She narrows her eyes. "Actually, on that note, did you clean my bathroom?"

A slow grin spreads over his face. "Made Matt do it."

Her jaw drops. Then she mutters, "Damn."

I take the side of the bed that's pressed up against the wall. I'm right below all the pictures of us she has stuck to her wall, and it makes me smile. Even when she was avoiding us, she couldn't bear to take them down.

It's a little tight having all three of us in Cora's bed, but I love the feeling of her soft, supple body pressed against mine. I run my hand over her curves as Wilder stands beside the bed, staring at us.

"What?" I ask.

He grins. "Reminds me of the sleepovers we had as kids before our parents stopped letting Cora join."

Snickering, I pull Cora closer to me. "Now look at us."

"Do you think they'll approve?" Cora asks. "Of us?"

As Wilder climbs into bed, he says, "Doesn't matter if they do. You're ours, Moonflower. And we're yours. Whether they approve or not doesn't change that."

"I know. I just want them to."

"Honestly? I wouldn't be surprised if they've been expecting it," Wilder replies. "Regardless, now isn't the time to worry about it. You need to sleep."

With a sigh, she settles in between us. We both wrap our arms around her, holding her close. And then we fall asleep, finally together and happy again.

Chapter Seven

Cora

I wake to an empty bed. At first it doesn't feel wrong because Matt normally gets out of bed before I do. But then I remember everything that happened last night, and a heavy weight settles on my chest.

Where are the boys?

Sitting up, I look around the room. Their bags are still on the floor, thank fuck. Not that I thought they would've left in the middle of the night. They love me too much to do that. Still, I was looking forward to waking up in their arms.

Maybe another time.

I get up, pulling on some clothes—leggings and a hoodie I stole from Wilder years ago. While I'm brushing my teeth, I give the bathroom a closer look. It's impressive, how clean Matt got it compared to last time.

I can't believe they made him clean it before they kicked him out.

Wilder is waiting in the hallway. He shoots me a glare.

"You're supposed to be asleep still."

"Um. Sorry? Why?"

Grabbing my arm, he pulls me into my room. "I was planning on waking you up."

The weight on my chest dissipates. *That's so sweet.* "I woke up alone."

"Exactly. That wasn't supposed to happen. I had a plan." With that, Wilder picks me up and throws me onto the bed.

I squeal as I land on my back. Wilder is on the mattress in a split second, grabbing my leggings and yanking them off me. My panties come down too, and then Wilder holds my legs open and stares down at me. With a squirm, I try to close my legs. But he spreads them further apart.

"Fucking beautiful," he murmurs. Then he lowers himself to his stomach and presses a kiss to my vulva.

"Wild," I moan.

"I should've done this last night," he says before circling my entrance with his tongue. His hands grip my thighs, pushing them apart as he nuzzles his face against me. "And then again before I even got out of bed."

"Where did you two go?" I say breathlessly as he continues teasing me.

"We were gonna make you breakfast. Then we decided to go out and get something instead. Ezra will be back soon."

"Oh. Where—"

He shushes me, finally lapping at my clit. The sparks his tongue shoots through my body are enough to shut me up. He's going slowly, like he's focusing on enjoying himself instead of making me come. But it still feels like heaven on earth.

"God, Wild, please don't stop."

He doesn't answer, too focused on what he's doing. As Wilder explores me with his mouth, my fingers curl into the messy sheets. He's groaning into me, holding onto my thighs like he's afraid I'll float away if he lets go. His movements are adoring and reverent, gentle and sweet. It's the opposite of how he was last night.

I move to take off my hoodie, but Wilder grabs my hands.

He lifts his head for a short moment, his eyes flicking to where his name is embroidered on the fabric right over my heart. "Keep it on. I like seeing my name on you."

After that, he doesn't let go of my hands, keeping them firmly in his grasp. He starts working me differently, concentrating more on my clit.

Tension builds in my belly—no, my whole body—as he starts bringing me closer to an orgasm.

Since he's not holding my legs open anymore, I wrap my thighs around his head. He groans, pressing his face into me. Then he sucks on my clit in a way that makes my eyes roll into the back of my head.

Everything about this feels right. Of course it does. We've all wanted it for so long. Not only that, but the three of us have always fit together so well. And now that we're finally done holding back, it's . . . well, it's so much more than I ever imagined.

I don't know how he does it, but it feels like Wilder is slowly pulling me apart. I can feel my orgasm coming the same way you can see a storm rolling in, so close but so far. Yet Wilder expertly inches me higher and higher, and I realize just how far I have to fall.

"Oh god, Wilder. Wilder, Wilder, *Wilder.*"

After that, my orgasm hits. It's like cresting the top of the hill of a roller coaster and then pausing for a split second before plunging into a dark tunnel. I can't help the scream that's ripped from my throat. I'm falling, falling, falling, and it feels like it'll never end.

It does, though. With one last lick, Wilder lifts his head. My legs fall to the mattress as I gulp in air.

Wilder's eyes are lit up with satisfaction. "You come really fucking hard."

"I don't always," I pant, propping myself up on my elbows.

He smirks. "You do now." Then he lowers his head again.

Wilder pulls two more orgasms from me like this. Each time I try to protest, he gives me a terrifying glare that says one thing and one thing only: *shut up and take it.*

He doesn't try to make me come quickly. No, he draws everything out, building up the tension in my body until I'm sure I'll burst at the seams. Only then does he shove me over the edge.

By the time I've come down from my third orgasm, I'm shaking, and my legs feel like jelly. I'm sweating in this hoodie, but Wilder won't let me take it off.

"Do you need water?" he asks, crawling over me and kissing me before I can answer. When he pulls away, I nod, too breathless to speak. "I'll be right back."

Once he's gone, I push myself into a sitting position, trying to process what just happened. I've come hard before, but *that* hard three times in a row? Never. And holy shit, I'm pretty sure Wilder didn't want to stop.

When Wilder comes back in with a glass of water, I meet him in the center of my room. I take a couple long sips while he runs his fingers through my tangled hair. Then he eases the glass from my hands and sets it on the nightstand.

There are many sides to Wilder—his playful side, his smart side, and his ridiculously hot, commanding, and dominant side. But right now, he looks so serious I'm almost afraid he's about to give me bad news.

Taking my face in his hands, Wilder leans his forehead against mine. His eyes fall closed, and for a moment we stay like that, perfectly silent. Then he whispers, "I love you, Cora Grimm. I have for years, and I was a fool for not making you mine years ago."

I fuse my mouth to his. I've missed him *so goddamn much.* If I'd come to my senses sooner—if I'd told them how I felt—maybe we could've reached this conclusion years earlier. But no, I had to keep my feelings and fears and doubts to myself. I may have him and Ezra now, but my heart aches for the three years we lost. That I ruined.

"I love you too," I say.

"Mmm. I know. Now get back on the bed. We're not done yet."

I don't move. Maybe it's silly, but I liked the way he threw me onto the bed. He raises an eyebrow at my defiance before he huffs out a laugh.

"You know, I always figured you liked it rough. I'm glad I was right."

I grin up at him. "I always hoped you did, too."

"Guess you got lucky then," he murmurs, his brown eyes darkening with desire. His gaze turns almost predatory as he scoops me up into his arms. "If you need a break, tap twice. On me, on the bed, wherever. I'll be paying attention."

"What? Need a break?"

Wilder answers by tossing me onto the mattress again. His body covers mine in an instant, his hands pinning my wrists to the sheets. As he takes my mouth in a controlling kiss, I arch into him and moan.

Oh my god. Why does it feel like this is meant to be? Like we're meant to be? *Fuck.* Who am I kidding. I've known it was meant to be for years.

"Wild," I pant when he pulls away.

"Get on your stomach," he says gruffly.

I scramble to obey him, flipping over. He forces my legs apart, making room for himself between them. I whimper when I hear him undoing his pants.

He leans over me, caging me into the bed. "You like it when I take control, pretty girl? You want me to fuck you into this mattress until you're so sore you're sobbing?"

Another whimper. "Yes."

He positions his dick at my entrance, barely slipping inside. "Do you trust me?"

"Of course I do, Wild."

He grabs the hair at the base of my neck. "Take a deep breath."

I do, and then Wilder shoves my face into my pillows at the same time he slams into me.

"Fuck," he shouts, pressing me down further. For a second, he stays inside of me, slowly pressing deeper. Then he pulls out, only to jerk his hips forward again. "Cora. Jesus Christ."

I can still breathe, but with my face buried in the pillows, I'm definitely not getting enough oxygen. It's an exhilarating feeling—one I've craved for years. Combined with Wilder pumping into me like a man possessed, my mind quickly tumbles into blissful ecstasy.

After a couple seconds, I realize I don't know how long I can stay like this without passing out. I don't think Wilder will hold me down for very long, but I'm not sure. Do I want him to make me faint? I don't think that'd be a good idea.

Leaning over me, Wilder groans right in my ear. "You feel so fucking good, Cora."

My cry is muffled and weak as he keeps a steady pace.

Wilder pulls me up, his lips feathering over my ear. "Too long?"

I gasp, oxygen flooding into my lungs. "No. Do it . . . do it again."

He pauses. "I need to look at you." He eases out of me and turns me onto my back. His hands slide under my hoodie, caressing the rolls of my stomach before squeezing my breasts. "You liked it?"

With a nod, I smile up at him. Then I tug at his shirt until he takes it off and I can stare at his bare chest. Something in my expression must indicate that I love seeing him halfway undressed for me, because he yanks the rest of his clothes off in an instant.

"If you need me to let up, tell me. I don't want to accidentally go too far."

"I'll tap." I perform the action then, tapping on the mattress twice.

That seems to be enough reassurance for him. He grabs my legs, opening them and getting into position. Again, he slides into me, letting out a low groan. Then he stares at the place we're connected—where he's seated as deeply in me as he can get. "I can't stop worrying this is all a dream," he says quietly. "That it's not real."

Sitting up as much as I can, I wrap one hand around the back of his neck. "It's real, Wild. I promise."

He blows out a breath, releasing some of the tension in his shoulders as he does. Then he kisses me, and it's so raw and desperate that a lump starts to form in my throat.

This is your fault. You put him through all that unnecessary pain.

"Wild, I'm so sor-"

He swallows up the rest of the sentence by grabbing my head and deepening the kiss. When he's done, he rests his forehead against mine, his eyes still closed.

"I won't do it again," I whisper.

He opens his eyes, and his stare is hard and demanding. "Damn right you won't. We won't fucking let you. You try to pull away from us again, I'll only come after you harder."

I tighten my grip on him. "I'm not running away."

"Good. And no man is ever touching you again, Moonflower. Just me and Ez. You understand?"

"I don't want anyone else."

That makes him smile. Not in a happy way, though. It's dark and possessive, which is exactly what I want from him right now.

Wilder pushes me down, placing his hands on either side of my head. "Open your mouth."

I do, swallowing after he spits into it.

"Pull your hoodie up."

I grab the fabric and push it up, leaving it bunched up at the top so he can see my breasts.

"Such a good girl," he mutters, adjusting the fabric with one hand so his name is still in view. "You ready?"

"Please," I whisper.

He keeps his thrusts slow and shallow at first, but I can see it in his eyes as he begins to lose control. His pupils dilate, and his nostrils flare when his willpower finally gives out. He groans, snapping his hips forward.

I cry out, grabbing onto his arms. "Do that again."

He does, grunting when I clench around his dick. God, he feels so good.

"Touch yourself, Cora," he says tightly. "Play with your clit the way you do when you're in bed at night thinking about me and Ez fucking you together."

With a moan, I obey. Wilder clamps a hand over my mouth, using his fingers to cover up my nostrils. I squeak in surprise.

"You said you wanted more, pretty girl. Did you change your mind?"

I shake my head, trying to inhale, but I can't. My brain starts to panic, but my body rides the high from relinquishing control.

"So trusting," Wilder says lowly. "My naive Moonflower, placing her life in my hands."

My eyes widen in shock. *Why does that sound like a threat?*

Wilder's gaze turns predatory as he watches me. "You're squeezing my dick so hard, you greedy little thing. You like it when I scare you?"

I do. God, I do. But all I can manage is another squeak. My body is officially panicking from the lack of air. Everything is getting a little fuzzy, and I'm not sure if I should tap out or try to go longer.

Wilder makes my mind up for me, removing his hand from my face. Breathing has never felt so sweet, so needed.

"Why . . . why did you stop?" I ask after a couple seconds.

"You weren't looking at me anymore. Weren't looking at anything, really." He pauses, still inside of me, and runs his hand through my hair. "Don't push yourself right to the edge."

I nod as my heartbeat slows. "Right. Got it."

He furrows his brows. "You good?"

"Yeah. That was just . . . um. Wow."

"I don't have to do it again."

"No, I want you to," I insist. "Please?"

He stares at me for a second, searching my face. "After a minute. I don't want to hurt you."

"Okay." I pull him down so his body is pressed against mine. Our lips meet immediately, and he starts moving inside of me again.

With him pressing into me, there isn't much room for me to keep rubbing my clit, but he tries to give me space. We stay like that for a while, until I get closer. I think he can sense it—probably because of the tension building in my body. There's no way he could miss it.

He gets up onto his knees, still leaning over me with his hands by my head. "Deep breath, Cora."

Giddiness and anticipation rush through me as I do what he says. And then his hand is clamped over my mouth and nostrils again. He picks up the pace of his thrusts, not taking his eyes off me.

Before, I could feel my orgasm creeping up on me. But now it's like it's chasing after me, so close I'm not sure why it hasn't hit me yet.

"Look at me, Moonflower," Wilder says, slamming into me repeatedly. "That's it. Now be a good girl and come for me so I can let you breathe."

With a whimper against his hand, I finally come. He releases me, and the sudden intake of air shoves me into a new level of orgasm I've never felt before. Everything feels more intense, like all of my senses are overloaded in the most pleasurable way. After a gasp, I cry out, clinging to Wilder's arms.

"Shit," he murmurs, still watching me. "I'm never fucking you in the dark again."

I can't respond. My orgasm knocked the breath—what little I had—out of me. So I just stare up at him with a dazed smile, panting and still clutching his arms.

He kisses in between my breasts, then around one of my nipples before licking it. He does the same to the other side before fusing his mouth to mine. After he pulls back, he says, "It's your turn."

"My turn?"

"To fuck me." Pulling out, he flops onto the bed next to me. "Give me all you've got, Moonflower."

I crawl on top of him. After I've slid down his cock, he runs his palms over my thighs to my stomach, where the hoodie has fallen down.

"Dammit. Take it off."

I pull it over my head, grinning at his reaction to seeing me fully naked. Then I start moving, up and down, savoring how he feels in this position.

"Fuck," he groans. "You have no idea how you look from this angle."

"Tell me," I whisper, grabbing his hands and placing them on my hips.

Squeezing the soft flesh there, he whispers, "Captivating. Every glorious inch of you, Cora."

I lean down and place my hands on his shoulders for balance. "That's . . . fuck, that's possibly the best compliment I've ever gotten."

His eyes are greedy as he takes me in. I always wondered how it would feel to be completely naked in front of him and Ezra. Of course I didn't think it would happen, but I still fantasized about it. Sometimes I imagined myself as a powerful seductress who could make them do anything I wanted. Which, let's be honest, isn't far from the truth.

Other times I worried I'd be insecure. I've known Wilder and Ezra since we were so small I can't remember life without them. In all that time, they've never seen me completely naked. But they've never made me feel uncomfortable about any aspect of who I am. So, I suppose, it's no surprise that as Wilder's gaze rakes over me hungrily, I bask in his attention.

Shaking his head, he says, "I have no idea how I've survived this long without having you on top of me like this."

With an eye roll, I say, "Probably because you don't actually need this."

"I do now," he says, his tone completely serious. One of his hands moves from my hip, and he uses his thumb to gently rub my clit.

I've already come four times, but apparently that isn't enough for him. He's looking at me like he's obsessed. Enraptured. Insatiable.

"I used to think about fucking you like this every morning," I say, staring down at him.

He moans. "So did I. Made me come so hard. But shit, Cora. This is so much better than my hand." To prove his point, he thrusts his hips upward, meeting my movements.

"Ooooh, oh god, Wild."

He repeats the motion, his eyes burning with greed again. It looks like he wants to take and take and take from me. And after all he's given this morning—hell, even without that—I'd let him take whatever he wants from me.

"Cora," he groans, pressing his head into the mattress. With his free hand, he reaches up and squeezes one of my breasts. He brushes his thumb over my nipple.

I can't help the gasp it pulls from me. Between that, him rubbing my clit, and me bouncing up and down on his dick, there's no way I can last long.

"I'm dragging you back home with us," he grits out, rolling his hips into me again. "I can't go a day without this."

Something about the way he says it pushes me over the edge. I think it's because it sounds like he actually means it—like he's not going to give me a choice. And while I want to finish out the school year here, I do love the thought of them kidnapping me.

"Fuck, *fuck,"* Wilder pants, holding onto me as I come.

It's hard to keep moving while my thoughts go blank, but I manage. I hold Wilder's gaze, relishing in the pure desperation on his features.

"Come for me, Wild," I say, squeezing his shoulders.

It takes another couple seconds, and then he's grabbing onto my thighs and choking out a groan. All of a sudden I get what he meant about never fucking me in the dark again. Last night, I could barely see him, and watching him come is addictive.

"Christ," he wheezes as he spills inside of me, filling me the way I've wanted him to for years. He stares up at me, eyes wide, showing a completely different side than the put-together, calm, secure version of himself that Wilder usually presents to the world.

I collapse next to him, pressing a clumsy kiss to his jaw.

"That was amazing, Cora," he murmurs. His hand strokes down my spine.

I hum in agreement, nestling into him. We fit perfectly together, and it makes me smile.

"Oh, shit. I should probably text Ez," Wilder says after a minute. He grabs his phone from the nightstand before rolling over to face me again. One of his hands rests on my side as he types away.

"Text him?"

He tosses his phone onto the mattress before pulling me into him. "He's been hanging out at the coffee shop he's bringing us breakfast from. We both wanted to make sure we got some alone time with you. You get him to yourself tomorrow morning."

The only way I can describe the emotions filling my chest is like watching a flower open in the sunlight. It's warm and full, and I know—I *know*—this is meant to be.

"Thank you," I whisper.

Wilder kisses me gently. "Of course."

We only stay in bed together for a couple minutes. I don't dare let my mind wander for a single second. I've wanted this for so long, and considering they're leaving tomorrow, I want to be present for every moment.

When Wilder gets up, I move to follow him, but he pushes me back onto the bed. He disappears for a minute, coming back with a wet washcloth.

"Open your legs."

"I can clean myself, Wild."

"Open your damn legs." He shoves them open, kneeling on the bed. Then he cleans me up gently. "I want to take care of you," he says quietly once he's finished.

I think he's trying to make me melt.

"Okay," I whisper.

The front door opens and closes, and we both perk up. Not only am I super hungry, but I want to see Ezra. So Wilder and I get dressed and then head into the kitchen.

I jump into Ezra's arms the moment I see him. He's dressed in classic Ezra Grey attire—dark, ripped jeans, a black hoodie with an illegible black metal band logo on it, and boots.

"Morning, Moonflower." Ezra plants a light kiss to my head while I tangle my fingers in his curls.

"Morning." I kiss up his neck and across his cheekbone before capturing his mouth with mine.

He smiles against my lips. "Missed me?"

I wouldn't trade the alone time I got with Wilder for anything, but of course I missed him. So I pull back and nod, staring into his deep brown eyes. "Always."

Disbelief flickers across his features, but only for a split second. Then he turns to the counter and grabs a to-go cup. "Pumpkin spice latte."

"Ooooh! You're the best." I grab it from him and take a sip, sighing with contentment.

"Got cinnamon rolls too."

"Jesus, Ez. You're gonna spoil her."

"I see nothing wrong with that," I say, grinning at both of them.

My kitchen table is too small for all three of us, so we eat in the kitchen. Wilder hoists himself up onto the counter. He leans back, sipping his coffee and watching us.

As I nibble on a cinnamon roll, that warm and giddy feeling comes back. The three of us have eaten countless meals together, but not as a couple. It puts a smile on my face that I can't get rid of.

Until Ezra pulls me back to reality, that is.

"How much homework do you need to get done today?" he asks.

My face falls. "Oh." To be honest, I've been so wrapped up in these two for the past twelve hours that I forgot about school. "I have a lot, actually."

"That's okay," he says. "I have some to finish up, too."

"And I've got a shit ton to work on," Wilder says tiredly.

I frown. When Wilder took the tutoring and content creation job, I worried it would be too much for him. But he likes it, and it gives him a job for after he's graduated.

"Don't worry about me, Cora," he says, forcing a smile. "I'll be fine."

As I start protesting, he slides off the counter and comes to stand right in front of me. I have to tilt my chin up to look at him. He kisses me, and I know it's just to shut me up, but if he's going to do it then this is definitely the way I prefer.

"One and a half more semesters," he says when he's done. "And then everything will get a hell of a lot better."

It's true, I hope. Our futures are all looking a little unstable right now, what with finding—and keeping—jobs that hopefully pay enough. Plus there's the possibility that we might not all be in the same city. Wilder can work from anywhere, and it depends on what Ezra does, but I have no idea where I'll end up.

"You look like you're panicking," Wilder says.

Ezra comes up behind me, placing his hands on my hips. Being sandwiched in between two men might make some people feel trapped, but with these two, all I feel is safe.

"I just want us to be happy," I mumble.

One and a half more semesters.

And then what? We graduate, and hopefully we move in together. But so many things could get in the way.

"We'll take it one step at a time, Moonflower," Ezra says.

Wilder nudges him. "Speaking of taking steps . . ."

Ezra goes stiff. "Shut up."

The corner of Wilder's mouth lifts up. "Never."

Ezra lets out something between a growl and a groan. I turn, placing my hands on his chest. The expression on his face is one of deep discomfort, and it breaks my heart seeing it.

"What's he talking about?"

He shrugs. "Don't worry about it."

"Don't worry about it?" Wilder snaps. "Ez! It's *very* worrying."

My stomach drops to the floor. "Ezra, what's going on?"

Chapter Eight

Ezra

Coming right off of promising not to hide things from each other by admitting that I've been doing just that is a horrible look. Ever since last night and agreeing we'd communicate with each other, I've known this conversation was coming. But dammit, I don't want to have it.

Cora knows about my depression. Of course she knows. But she has no idea how much it's affected me.

"Ezra," she says softly, tugging on my shirt.

Sighing, I lean my forehead against hers. What if she looks at me differently after this? Half the time Wilder is the only reason I somehow manage to stay alive. He's always reminding me to eat and making sure there are easy-to-prepare meals in the apartment.

When things get especially bad, he's the one who drags me out of bed. He's the one who's always down to go on a walk with me or talk or do literally anything if he thinks there's a chance it'll make me feel better.

I know Cora will understand. But this is different, you know? How could she be attracted to someone who can't find the motivation to get out of bed some days? Hell, I usually don't even want to exist.

"Cora." I run my fingers through her soft curls. *Fuck, I don't want her to take this the wrong way. What if she feels like it's because she's not enough for me?* "I love you. You know I love you."

She nods, smiling even though her brown eyes are full of worry and her brows are furrowed.

"But I . . . Sometimes I don't want to . . ."

"Be alive?" she whispers.

I nod.

"I already know that." She chews on her lip for a moment, and then it clicks. "It's gotten worse?"

"That's one way to put it," I mumble.

"Yes," Wilder butts in. "It's gotten so much fucking worse."

Cora's shoulders sag. "You never went to the therapist I told you about?"

"No." I can't look at her. Can't do it. I know she'll be disappointed, and I just can't face it.

Wilder stays silent, watching us both. No doubt, he's already sick of this conversation. How many times has he tried—and failed—to drill into my brain all the things Cora has tried to tell me in the past? Too many.

Cora cups my face in her hands, forcing me to meet her gaze. "I know it's hard, Ez."

I grit my teeth. Her first couple years here, Cora struggled with making friends. A lot of it had to do with a lack of motivation to take care of herself. To do anything, really. She's struggled with depression since we were teens. Moving away from home was a huge adjustment for her, and it made her downspiral pretty hard our freshman year.

It was around then that she started avoiding me and Wilder. We were worried as hell, but we weren't sure what to do. And any attempts we made to get her to open up usually backfired.

I remember being so frustrated that I wanted to drive out here, corner her, and force her to spit out what she was thinking. So I can only imagine her and Wilder feel a similar way about me now.

"Therapy can be scary, I get it," Cora says. "And so can meds. I'm not saying you have to do either of those things. But . . . maybe we can come up with something?"

Cora's eyes are wide and so full of concern I'm afraid she might start crying. I get it. Hearing that someone you love is depressed is scary.

"All right," I mutter. "We will."

And I mean it, too. It's not like I enjoy being miserable. The thought of being happy just seems so far off. Even the concept of being at peace—with myself, our future, life in general, everything—seems virtually impossible.

"You know she doesn't look at you differently because of this, right?" Wilder says. His voice is firm, but not in an impatient way. He's worried—probably rightly so.

When I don't reply, Cora wraps her arms tight around my torso. "Who you are is who you are. That doesn't change because you're depressed. I'd never love you less because of it."

"Maybe I'm not the same person," I mumble.

She frowns. "What do you mean?"

"I don't . . . I'm *not* the same. I haven't drawn in weeks. Half the time I barely eat. My sleep schedule is a mess, I don't care about school anymore, and I rarely have energy to do anything more than the bare minimum."

"That doesn't change who you are," she says gently. "You're still the thoughtful, sweet, introspective boy I've always known. Just look, you *drove five hours* yesterday to surprise me for the weekend."

"That was Wild's idea," I mutter.

"And whose idea was it to get me cinnamon rolls and a pumpkin spice latte?"

"Not mine," Wilder says.

Cora beams up at me. "See? Not only did you remember I love both of those, but you thought to get them for me. That's a very Ezra Grey thing to do. So you're still in there, I promise. And I'll love you no matter what. Forever, Ez."

I sigh. I can't stop worrying that she's wrong. What if I get worse instead of better? What if I end up dragging her and Wilder down with me? There's a chance she'd be better off with just him and not me.

That's not what any of us want, though. And I already know how pissed Wilder will get if I bring it up again. So I nod and kiss Cora on the forehead. "Okay."

"I vote you call your doctor on Monday to make an appointment," Wilder says.

Cora glances up at me questioningly. It's just like her to not want to push me to the point of discomfort. Wilder, on the other hand, has seen me every day. He tries to hide how worried he is, but it bleeds through when he thinks I'm not paying attention. It makes sense that he wants me to do something ASAP.

"I don't have to call," I reply. "I can just book an appointment online."

"Do you . . . want to?" Cora asks.

"I don't want anything." *Fuck.* "Except you."

"But are you okay with it? Talking to your doctor about getting on meds?"

"I'm not against it." *And maybe it'll help me feel human again.*

"Then we're scheduling it right now," Wilder says. "Get your laptop out."

I don't protest, grabbing it from my bag in Cora's room. Let's face it—I should've done this months ago. And if someone doesn't force me to schedule the appointment, I'll probably put it off for months. I'm not proud of that, but it's the damn truth.

Cora and Wilder sit on either side of me as I schedule the appointment. The next available time is a couple weeks away, and it fits around my class schedule, so I choose that one.

Once I'm done, Cora releases a long breath and takes my hands in hers. "It took me months to do anything about my depression when I moved away. I know how hard it is, Ez, so I'm proud of you for doing this."

"Be proud of me after I've gone to the appointment."

With a smile, she shakes her head. "I can be proud of you for both."

"I'm proud of you, too," Wilder says quietly. "And relieved, if I'm being honest."

I think I might be, too.

Cora wraps her arms around me, and after a second Wilder does as well. Everything in me screams that I should be uncomfortable with this, that there's no way they could be so accepting. But then Cora presses a soft kiss to my neck.

"One step at a time," she whispers.

Wilder nods. "And we'll be here with you the whole time."

Finally, I relax. "Thanks, guys."

"I'll do anything I can to help," Cora says. "Even if you need to call me and talk about things you've told me about a thousand times. I'll listen again."

"I know you would," I murmur.

She smiles. "Good."

After that, we all settle on the couch together, either working or getting school done. We have a lot to get done, especially since Wilder told me earlier that he has plans for tonight. I think Cora will love what he has in store.

For a second, I stare at both of them. Cora is writing while glancing between her textbook and notebook, and Wilder is typing away on his laptop. I could get used to afternoons like this.

"I love you. Both of you."

They both look up from their work.

"Love you too, Ez," Wilder says.

Cora grins. "A lot."

Yep—that helps. It's not just that I know how they feel. It's that we're together again, even if we're all focused on our own things. It makes me happy.

And having that appointment scheduled helps some, too. I actually *did* something to help myself. It may be small, but it feels like a huge weight off my shoulders.

After another minute of secretly watching them study, I turn back to my laptop. This homework isn't gonna do itself. And I need to get it done so I can be fully focused for tonight.

Chapter Nine

Cora

"Where are we going?" I ask.

After dark, the boys blindfolded me and put me in the back of Wilder's car. We've been driving for what feels like a half hour, and they won't tell me anything.

"You'll find out soon enough," Wilder says from the driver's seat. His voice gives away nothing—no hints of excitement or mischief or lust.

Groaning, I slouch down. The last thing I want is for someone to see me and think they're actually kidnapping me. Thankfully it's dark enough no one should be able to see into the windows.

Eventually, we come to a stop. One of the guys gets out, and then I hear my door opening. Someone—Wilder, if the smell of his leather jacket is any indicator—leans over me and undoes my seatbelt.

"Time to walk, pretty girl."

After helping me out of the car, he closes the door.

"Where are we?" I say. A slight breeze blows through my clothes, so we aren't in a garage or something. But other than that, I'm clueless.

"I want you to know something, Moonflower. If you express that you want something, Ezra and I will find a way to give it to you. Always. You understand?"

"I do."

What the hell is that supposed to mean? I've expressed that I want a lot of things. Especially if I include that second blog post Wilder read.

He guides me to . . . I don't know where. My foot catches on something, but Wilder keeps me upright. Or is it Ezra?

"Ez?"

Silence.

"Where's Ezra?"

"Don't worry about it." There's something almost predatory about the way Wilder says it.

Dread courses through my veins, but it's quickly followed by a tentative sense of delight and anticipation. "Wilder . . ."

"You scared, my pretty Moonflower?" He shoves me forward harder, almost making me trip.

"Y-yes."

"Good."

We walk in silence for another minute. Leaves crunch under our feet, and I hear a couple twigs snap, too.

"Are we in the woods?"

"Maybe."

"In the . . . in the dark?"

He chuckles, a low and dangerous sound. Then he stops me, and I feel his fingers brushing against my hair as he undoes my blindfold.

I was right—we're in the woods. The moon is visible through the barren branches that extend upward and sideways at crooked angles.

A rustling noise comes from my right, and I jump.

Wilder doesn't move to comfort me or tell me I'm safe, and it makes my skin break out in goosebumps. When I turn to face him, he's grinning. But it's not a happy grin. No, it's creepy as hell. Almost sinister.

I gulp. "Why did you bring me here?"

"To chase you."

Oh god.

"Chase me."

"That's right." He steps up to me, his fingers feathering down my arms. "You're going to run, and when I catch you—because you will *never* be able to get away from me, Moonflower—I'm going to shove you to the ground and fuck you. You want that, right?"

Butterflies come to life in my stomach. "You read my blog post, you know I do."

He grips my chin, forcing me to look up at him. "I want you to say it."

"Yes," I whisper. "I do."

"Tell me what else you'd like."

"I . . ." My cheeks heat, and I'm grateful the darkness conceals my blush. I've never voiced this desire out loud, and I have no idea if it'd even be something Wilder would want. But he and Ezra made it clear that they won't judge me.

And Wilder already knows what I'm dying to say. I just have to build up the courage to actually say it.

"Spit it out, Cora."

"I want to pretend I don't want it." I pause. "If you're into that."

"There's nothing I want more than to fulfill all the fantasies in that pretty head of yours." As he says it, he moves to stand behind me. His hands rest possessively on my hips, making the ache in between my legs worse. "You want to be scared?"

"Yes." I hesitate again. "I know it's dark." I hate the way my voice trembles.

"The darker the better, my lovely Moonflower."

"You're sure?" I whisper.

He squeezes my hips. "Perfectly. Anything off limits?"

"No."

He chuckles. "Good."

"So I'm going to . . . run?"

"Mmhmm."

"Do I get a head start?"

"Of course. Don't want to catch you too fast." He brushes his lips down my neck.

"Where's Ezra?"

"You'll find out."

That sends a shiver of delight through me.

"Your safe word is pumpkin."

"Pumpkin?"

"That's right. And if you can't speak, tap twice. Anywhere."

I gulp. How many times have I imagined him doing that? How many times have I come from the thought alone? An embarrassing amount, if I'm being honest.

"Ready, Cora?"

I swallow. "Yes."

Wilder turns me slightly so I'm facing right in between two trees. He places his lips right next to my ear, his voice a low rumble. "Run."

He releases me, and I take off. Thankfully the moonlight helps illuminate the forest some, so I'm able to see most fallen branches.

I don't dare look back. Wilder said he'd give me a head start, but I don't know how long that'll be. Trying to gauge how far away he is will just slow me down. Or worse, it'll make me trip and fall.

As I run through the trees, my chest tightens, and my heart feels like it's in my throat. I know it's fake—Wilder would never hurt me. Well, he wouldn't hurt me *too much*. But it feels so real.

Running through the forest is scary as hell, too. I can see, but only barely. Every snap of a twig or rustle of leaves has me jumping out of my skin.

And then I hear it—a deep, unhinged laugh that echoes through the trees. When it reaches my ears, I start running faster.

"You can't hide from me, pretty girl," Wilder calls.

With a gasp, I veer to my right. Can he see me? Or am I far ahead enough? I narrowly avoid scraping up against a tree as I risk a glance behind me. It's not worth it—I don't see him.

Footsteps sound behind me and to my right, so I start heading in my original direction. *How has he caught up so fast?*

Wilder laughs again. "You think you can outrun me?"

I don't respond. Just in case he can't see me, I don't want to give away where I am.

With every step I take, I try to ready myself for his hands reaching through the darkness and grabbing me. Will he tackle me to the ground? Or will he pin me to a tree? Or maybe he'll grab my arm? Will it hurt?

"Slowing down already, Moonflower?" Wilder's voice is unnervingly close.

With a gasp, I realize I've lost my pace. I force my legs to move faster, whimpering when he snickers behind me. He doesn't sound close enough to reach me—*yet*. Is he intentionally keeping his distance? I can't tell.

I burst out the other side of the woods, which I wasn't expecting. The lack of trees gives me more light, but it also means I'm more exposed to Wilder.

It takes me a second to recognize the dark shapes in front of me. Rectangles, pillars, and crosses are all scattered across the space in front of me, and behind them all is a small church.

A graveyard. I'm in a graveyard.

I dodge between the tombstones, ducking behind one that's taller than I am. For a second, I let myself heave in a few breaths. I'm caught between wanting to draw this out and wanting Wilder to find me. The thrill of not knowing when he'll catch me has my body tingling with adrenaline. But I'm also desperate to feel him against me.

"Go ahead and hide, Cora. I'll find you eventually."

There's something about the way his voice echoes through the grave-yard that has me shivering. It sounds like Wilder is to my left, so I move to my right, creeping through the tombstones. When I hear him laugh behind me, I break into a run.

The shadows are long and creepy, stretching out almost like death itself is trying to wrap around my ankles and pull me into the ground. The thought sends goosebumps across my skin, and I start running faster. Wilder's footsteps pound on the grass behind me, getting closer and closer.

Oh god. Oh god oh god oh god. He's so close.

There's an obelisk up ahead. If I can get around it, maybe I can lose him. And then—

A tall figure steps out from behind the obelisk, shrouded in a black cloak and holding a long, deadly scythe. His face is darkened by his hood, presenting a silhouette I'd recognize anywhere.

The Grim fucking Reaper.

I can't help my scream. I can't stop, either. Of course I try, but I slip on the damp grass, tumbling right into him. His arm locks around me like a vise.

With another scream, I push against him, but then someone comes up behind me, caging me between both of them.

Their bodies are familiar against me, but I still struggle. "Let me go," I shout, my voice desperate and wobbly. It's the last thing I get out before a hand is clamped over my mouth.

"I told you that you couldn't run from me," Wilder says lowly in my ear. He presses into me from behind, chuckling at my pitiful whimpers. "Awww, are you afraid, pretty girl?"

When I try to break their hold on me, they only grip me harder. My breaths are short and shallow, and the cold air burns my lungs.

"You're so pretty when you're scared," Ezra murmurs. While his hood hides his grin, I can hear it in his voice, and it sends a chill deep into my bones. He brings the tip of the scythe under my chin, forcing me to tilt my head up. Up close, I can see that it's just a prop—not sharp at all—but from a distance it looked so *real*.

Wilder nips at my earlobe, making me jump. I can't move, can't speak, and I'm barely able to catch my breath. Yet I can feel the heat blooming in between my legs and spreading through my body. My skin tingles as I can just barely make out Ezra's eyes underneath his hood. They're dark and predatory, glittering with lust.

Again, I whimper. I try to beg them to let me go, but the words come out muffled and disconnected against Wilder's palm. So I lunge to the side in an attempt to run. They don't let me, though.

"Oh, you're not going anywhere," Ezra says. "You belong to us now, Cora, and we're never letting you go."

In one swift motion, he throws his scythe to the ground and drops his hood. He rips Wilder's hand away and fuses his mouth to mine, kissing me so roughly I squeak in shock. I'm still not used to Ezra being anything but gentle with me, but if I'm being honest, it feels natural.

Ezra undoes my pants, yanking the zipper down and shoving his hand into my underwear. He groans when he feels how wet I am.

"No," I sob. Even though I know it's futile, I try to break out of their hold again.

"You're protesting, but you're soaked," Ezra says. His fingers drift from my entrance to my clit, spreading my arousal. They slide easily because he's right—I'm so drenched I can feel it.

Still, I fight against them, even as Ezra circles my clit in a way that has my knees threatening to buckle. Wilder brings his hand back over my mouth, making sure to block my nostrils as well.

I scream, but the sound doesn't carry far.

"You want to breathe, pretty girl?"

I nod.

"Then stay still."

My body is trembling, but I stop fighting.

"Good girl," Wilder says, sweetly yet condescendingly. He doesn't move his hand.

Panic rises in my chest. I almost start struggling again, but I have a feeling Wilder wouldn't like that. My muscles seize up, both from the lack of oxygen and from Ezra working my clit. Finally, Wilder removes his hand. I gasp for air, clinging to Ezra's hoodie.

"She got even wetter when you took away her ability to breathe, Wild. What does that say about you, Moonflower?"

"Our girl likes having her power stripped away from her. Don't you?" Wilder says. He yanks my tank top up, taking my bra with it. My nipples harden instantly when the cool air hits them.

Ezra groans. "Look at you. Fucking perfect."

Wilder squeezes my breasts, kneading them and teasing my nipples.

"No," I whimper. I try to shy away, but there's nowhere to go.

"What did I tell you about struggling?" Wilder pinches my nipples hard enough I wouldn't be surprised if he drew blood.

I cry out. Tears spring into my eyes, and I can't help it—I start fighting again.

"That's it," Wilder grits out. One of his hands leaves my body, coming up against my mouth and my nose again. He holds it there, not letting me breathe, while he plays with my breasts with his other hand.

This whole time, Ezra has had one of his arms around my lower waist, holding me firmly in place. His fingers dig into my skin until I settle down again.

Ezra clicks his tongue, watching tears fall onto my cheeks. "You made your pretty girl cry, Wild." He circles my clit faster, adding a touch more pressure. When I grunt against Wilder's hand, he grins. "What should we do with her when we're done? Tie her up and throw her in the river?"

I squeak in protest.

"Maybe we should bury her with all these old skeletons," Wilder replies. "Who'd find her here?"

My thoughts are getting muddy and slow from the lack of oxygen. They have me shaking, trapped, and terrified—exactly like they want. Exactly like *I* want. And I don't think I can hold on for much longer. The tension rising in my body is almost at an unbearable point.

I let out a muffled sob, blinking more tears from my eyes. Ezra leans down and licks them away. His fingers slip inside of me, his thumb rubbing against my clit, and it rips a choked noise from me.

"So tense," he murmurs. "So breakable."

I moan. Because right now, all I want is to break. For *them* to break me. So close. *So fucking close.*

Just as I think I'm about to pass out, Ezra curls his fingers into me. It's exactly what I need to push me over the edge. I hear a weak whine, and it takes a moment to register that it came from me.

As I begin to come, Wilder releases me, and I heave in a breath. The sudden rush of oxygen pushes my orgasm to new heights, just like earlier except *more.* I groan, and my legs give out, but they don't let me fall.

"Shit," Ezra whispers, working my clit with a feather-light touch. He lets me take a couple breaths, watching me with rapt fascination. Then he grabs the hair at the base of my neck, angling my face upward, and slams his lips to mine.

Wilder holds me up as Ezra plunders my mouth. He bites my bottom lip until I taste blood, and then he licks it away with a groan. I grab onto his shoulders, slowly regaining my footing as he starts moving his fingers inside of me again.

Once I'm standing on my own again, Wilder moves away from me. The absence of heat against my back sends a shiver down my spine. Then I yelp when he yanks my jeans and panties down my legs, leaving them around my knees. He smacks my ass once, twice, before he pulls me away from Ezra.

With his hands on my shoulders, Wilder shoves me to the ground. I fall forward, catching myself with my hands. But then Wilder grabs my hair and yanks me up so I'm on my knees.

"Get her shirt off," he tells Ezra.

I expect Wilder to let go of my hair so Ezra can pull my shirt over my head. But instead, Ezra kneels in front of me and gently traces a finger down my stomach. He slips my flannel off my shoulders, letting it fall into the grass. Then he takes two fistfuls of my tank top and yanks.

The sound of fabric ripping fills the air, and I gasp. Ezra tears my tank top apart until it's nothing more than a shredded heap on the ground. Then he unclasps my bra and discards it, throwing it onto a flat tombstone.

"Ezra!"

"What? It's the most excitement that—" He pauses, leaning over to get a better look at the stone. "—Francis Hendricks has seen in a long time."

I'm blushing furiously, but either Ezra can't see or he doesn't care.

"Get down," Wilder says, shoving me forward.

I catch myself with my hands, but then Wilder grabs my arms and yanks them behind me. I fall to the ground, my cheek hitting the wet grass. My ass is exposed and sticking up in the air, and Wilder is kneeling behind me, his legs on either side of mine. The tip of his cock slides against my clit.

"God," I whisper.

Wilder laughs, snapping his hips forward. "He's not here, little Moonflower. You know that."

Chapter Ten

Wilder

Cora screams as I slam into her. It's a bewitching sound, one I'm planning on wrenching out of her daily for the rest of our lives. When I pull out, she whimpers, my name a breathless plea on her lips.

"What do you want?" I smack her ass, watching it jiggle in the most perfect way.

She's not scared anymore, nor is she struggling. Our precious Moonflower is quivering and soaked and desperate for more.

"You," she moans. "Please fuck me. Please, Wilder."

"Mmm. Ez, don't you love how quickly she went from struggling against us to begging for us? Not much of a fighter, is she?"

Ezra chuckles. "No, no she's not."

Cora pushes against me, taking my cock an inch or two. I grab her hips and push her forward, making her whine.

"Pathetic," I chide.

She sniffles. But then she groans when I slide into her all the way to the hilt. *Shit,* she feels good. But I want her to struggle more, and I know she wants it, too.

I pull out. "Get over the tombstone." I point to the one Ezra threw her bra onto. It's flat, flush with the grass, so it won't be too uncomfortable.

"Wh-what?" Cora gets onto her hands and her knees, but she doesn't move.

"We're going to fuck you over the tombstone. Crawl."

"But that's—"

"Disrespectful as hell? Yeah, it is. Now get moving." I slap her ass, making her yelp.

But she still doesn't move.

She glances between me and Ezra, her eyes wide. When she realizes just how serious I am, her face goes slack with fear. Yet she rubs her thighs together, letting out a moan so quiet I almost don't hear it.

With a huff, I stand. She starts to crawl—away from me *and* away from the tombstone. It's a little awkward considering her jeans are still only half-off, keeping her knees together.

"Oh, that's a bad idea, Moonflower."

She screams when I grab her legs and yank. She falls to her stomach, trying to grab onto a tombstone to resist me. It's a pointless move. I'm much stronger than she is.

"No, no, don't!" she begs.

I drag her toward the tombstone, grinning when she starts kicking. "That's more like it."

"No," she shrieks.

Ezra holds up a hand for me to stop, so I do. "You remember your safe word, Cora?"

After Cora started running from me, I sent Ezra a quick text updating him on what Cora wanted and giving him her safe word.

"Yes," she says, heaving in short, hard breaths.

He lets his hand drop. "Okay. Just wanted to make sure."

Since my grip on Cora's legs went slack, she takes the opportunity to lunge out of my grasp. She only gets a few feet before Ezra blocks her. We scoop her up, carrying her to the tombstone and setting her on the ground roughly.

Cora scrambles to her hands and knees, but Ezra keeps a tight grip on her hair. She freezes, letting out a sound that's somewhere between a moan and a whine. I waste no time getting behind her and guiding my cock to her entrance.

She tries to slide out of my hold, but I keep a firm grip on her hips so I can move her how I want. Then I slam into her, groaning at the feeling of her clenching around my dick.

Cora cries out, grabbing onto Ezra's cloak with one hand. "Wilder!"

"Someone's going to hear you, pretty girl."

"Stop," she sobs.

"Mmm, I don't think I will," I say, and I swear I feel wetness gushing from her at my words. I keep up a punishing pace, relishing in the softness of her thighs against my own.

After she screams again, Ezra pulls her head up by her hair. "We gave you a chance, Moonflower. You blew it."

"W-what?" she whispers.

But he's already lifting his cloak up to undo his pants. Once he's freed his cock, he slaps it across her face. "If you can't shut up, we'll fucking make you. Open up."

She hesitates, so I smack her ass. "You won't like what we'll do if you don't listen."

With another sob, she takes Ezra's cock into her mouth. He groans while she sucks, working her way up and down his dick. I'm surprised he doesn't try to take control, but maybe he doesn't want to overwhelm her too much right now. As Cora takes him down her throat, she moans, and I laugh.

"You like this, don't you?" I taunt. "You're gonna get off to us fucking you over some old man's grave."

She makes a horrified noise.

"Such a naughty girl."

She bucks against me before she moves off Ezra's dick, gasping for air.

"Say it, Moonflower. Say what you are."

"I—I . . . I can't," she pleads.

"I don't believe you. Do you, Ezra?"

"No. What are you, Cora?"

She lowers her head, crying into the grass. And then, "I'm your naughty Moonflower."

I smile down at her even though she can't see. "Damn right you are," I murmur, stroking the curve of her hip.

The gentle caress makes her relax into me. I let her keep her false sense of safety for another second before I smack her ass so hard I can just barely make out the pink handprint on her skin in the dark. She jerks her body away from me, so I grab onto her again and snap my hips forward.

She cries out again, so Ezra grips her jaw, forcing it open and sliding his dick back into her mouth. This time, he doesn't stay so still, hitting the back of her throat and making her gag.

"I told you to stay *quiet,* Cora," he grits out.

I keep pumping into her while Ezra thrusts into Cora's mouth. His movements are somewhere between gentle and harsh while he lets her maintain some semblance of control. But he pulls out of her mouth after a minute, letting go of her hair.

"You gonna stay quiet?"

She nods, sniffling and coughing.

"Good girl." He strokes her hair before tucking his dick in his pants and letting his cloak fall. Then he crawls so he's by her side, kneeling next to the tombstone. Snaking a hand in between her legs, he groans when he feels how soaked she is.

Cora gasps when I assume Ezra finds her clit. Then she groans grudgingly.

"Are you going to come on my cock, pretty girl?"

"No," she moans in the most unconvincing way.

I laugh. "You will, mark my words. And then you're gonna come on Ezra's. No escaping it."

"Shiiiiiiit," she whines.

I keep my thrusts hard and unrelenting. By the time she's on the edge, the sound of skin slapping against skin is so loud I swear everyone within a mile radius can hear. Not to mention her screams.

"Wild, I'm so close," Cora pants. "Ezra . . . Ez, fuck."

Shit. I dig my fingernails into her skin. It's not hard enough to draw blood, but it's enough to shove her over the edge.

At first, her whole body tenses. Then she lets out a breathless groan as she comes. And fuck does it feel good, having her fall apart while she's wrapped around my dick.

"Never letting you go," I mutter. "Can't. Fucking can't."

A choked sound escapes her throat. I don't slow down, forcing her higher until she screams. Only when Ezra removes his hand does she come down.

For the past minute or so, I've been trying to keep myself from coming prematurely. So now, I let myself go, releasing into her with a curse. She pushes against me, taking everything I have to give.

When I pull out, I let go of her wrists. She falls to her side, collapsing into Ezra. He gathers her up in his arms, shifting so he's sitting on his ass and she's in his lap.

Stroking her hair out of her face, he smiles down at her. It's gentle and caring, which I think is ironic considering he's about to destroy her.

Cora moans, reaching out for me and taking my hand. The simple action—no, the fact that she still wants me close even though she's in Ezra's arms—fills my heart to the brim.

I grab Cora's face and capture her mouth in a long, hard kiss. *Mine.* She may be Ezra's too, but she's also *mine.* Forever. Fucking forever.

When I pull away, she goes limp with a happy sigh.

Ezra snorts. "We're not done yet, Moonflower."

"Do you want me to fight?" she whispers.

He shakes his head, kissing her forehead. "No. But I'm not going to go easy on you."

"I don't want easy."

This time when he smiles at her, it's dark and lustful. "That's my girl. Wild, pull her pants off."

I do, taking off her boots first and then stripping her bare. We both take in the lushness of her body, and I stroke down her perfect thighs.

"Get up, Cora," Ezra says.

I help her to her feet, snickering at how wobbly she is. I fucking wrecked her. And god, I can't wait to do it again.

He leads her down the row of tombstones and to a large stone cross that's taller than she is. With a smirk, I gather up Cora's clothes and boots.

"Ezra." She says it in protest, but she still lets him place her against it. "We're going to hell for this."

"Sounds better than heaven to me. Now get on your knees."

She gives him a confused look. "Facing you? Or facing the cross?"

"Me, Moonflower. The only person you'll worship tonight is me, and then I'm going to worship you."

Cora lowers herself to her knees. She's shivering, but she doesn't complain. Instead, she focuses on undoing Ezra's pants and pulling his cock out.

Running a hand through her hair, he steps closer to her. Cora licks her lips before running her tongue along the underside of his dick. One of her hands rests on his thigh, and she uses the other to stroke him as she sucks on the tip of his cock.

"No hands, Moonflower. Just your mouth."

She obliges, folding both hands in her lap.

"Such a good girl," Ezra murmurs as she takes as much of him into her mouth as she can.

As Cora continues to work up and down his dick, he leans forward and grabs onto the cross for balance. I can see just how tense he is, how hard it is for him to hold back so she can have control. We'll see how long he lasts.

"I'm a fool for not having you do this years ago, Cora. Christ." One of his hands drops to her head, fisting the hair at the back of her neck.

She lets out a squeak, working harder, like she knows what's coming. Her head moves faster, and she tries to take him so deep that she gags.

"Fuck," Ezra groans as she blinks back tears. He yanks her forward.

Cora chokes, but he makes no move to give her a reprieve. Only when she digs her nails into his jeans does he let her move off his dick. She coughs and gasps, but then she smiles.

"Shit. You love it when I do that, don't you?"

She replies by opening her mouth wide and sticking her tongue out.

"My pretty Moonflower. God, I love you so much."

She melts, pressing a tiny kiss to the tip of his cock. Then she goes back to keeping her mouth open while staring up at him with those enchanting eyes of hers.

Fuck. This is the type of thing I never want to forget. I'd take a picture, or even a video, but I'd never do that without their permission. Still, though. This is fucking hot.

"Scooch back, Cora. That's it. Lean against the headstone. Perfect. Now I'm going to fuck this pretty face of yours. You ready?"

She nods, keeping the back of her head against the cross. When he runs the tip of his cock over her lips, she captures it in her mouth and sucks.

"So eager," he says with a smirk. Then, with one hand gripping the cross and the other holding the back of her neck, he jerks his hips forward.

He said he wouldn't be gentle, and he holds to his promise. Ezra fucks Cora's face as hard as I know he's wanted to for years. She takes him without fighting, getting in short breaths when she can. Every time she gags, Ezra groans and grips the cross harder.

After a minute, he pulls out. Cora heaves in a breath as drool falls from her chin. Her eyes are unfocused and hazy, and her tear-coated cheeks glint in the moonlight. It shows off just how ruined her makeup is. *Beautiful. Fucking beautiful.*

Ezra gives her a small break, and then he's at it again. He groans as he fucks her mouth the way he'd fuck either of her other pretty holes. As his thrusts get more and more unrelenting, Cora chokes and struggles for air.

"Eyes up here, beautiful," he says.

She looks up at him as tears stream down her cheeks. He pulls out again to let her breathe, and a small, feminine whimper comes from her throat.

"You're taking my dick so well," he murmurs, stroking her hair. "Can you handle more?"

"Please," she whispers.

"Just for a little while. I'm not coming down your throat tonight."

She moans at the thought, giving him a pleading look.

He shakes his head. "Maybe tomorrow. Now open that mouth wide for me."

I've never been one to gravitate toward watching. Nothing against it, just never really got the appeal. But right now, as Ezra pumps into Cora's mouth with abandon, I realize this might be my new favorite thing to do. Aside from fucking her myself, that is.

There's just something about the way she willingly surrenders herself over to us. Maybe it's the absolute trust, or maybe it's that I've loved her since we were kids. But seeing Cora shoved up against the cross like this, messy and wrecked and gagging on Ezra's cock . . . yeah. I fucking love it.

When Ezra pulls out this time, Cora slumps against the tombstone. He drops to his knees in front of her, smiling and stroking her hair.

"Wild," he says, "hand me her tank top."

I do, and he gently wipes away the drool from her chin and mouth. Then he kisses the tip of her nose. "You take my cock so prettily, Moonflower."

"I want more, Ez," she begs.

"You'll get it. But first, I need you to stand up."

He helps her stand, keeping an arm around her as he pushes her against the cross. She curls into him, shivering. God, her teeth are chattering.

"You want your flannel?"

She nods.

Ezra takes it from me, saying, "You can wear it, but it stays open. I want to see you." He runs a hand down her side before helping her put her shirt on. "Your body is too fucking beautiful to hide."

She smiles up at him, eyes shining. Then he kisses her gently, eating up her little sigh of contentment. From what I can tell, she loves how he goes from fucking her like he hates her to treating her like she's the most precious thing in the world.

Hell, even I think it's sweet. I don't know what put the thought in his head that she wouldn't want him. Especially with the way she's clinging to him right now.

When Ezra breaks off the kiss, he gets to his knees in front of her. "Spread your legs for me."

She does, gasping when he puts one of her legs over his shoulder. She runs one of her hands through his curls. When Ezra presses small, worshipful kisses to the stretch marks on her inner thighs, she tugs on his hair with a moan.

Finally, he places his mouth directly in between her legs and sucks. Her hand tightens in his hair, and she grinds against his face with a whimper.

"You like that, my beautiful Moonflower?"

"I—I think about this all the time."

"What, me eating you out?"

She shakes her head. "Me playing with your hair. While . . . while you do this."

He pulls back slightly, his gaze boring into hers. "Is that why you reacted so strangely when you saw I grew out my hair?"

"Maybe."

"Were you thinking about it then? On that video call? Were you thinking of me sucking on this pretty clit of yours while you had your fingers in my hair?"

With a whimper, she nods. "I like your curls."

"Fuck," he whispers. "What are you waiting for, then?"

She twists her fingers into his curls with a bashful, moonlit smile. It's sweet—cute, even.

"Both of them," Ezra snaps. "Both hands. Now, Cora."

She obeys in an instant, fisting his curls and tugging. With a groan, Ezra buries his face in between her legs. I watch as she throws her head back, hitting the cross so hard it probably hurts. But she's so distracted by Ezra's ministrations, I'm not sure the pain even registers in her mind.

"Ez," she moans. "Ezra, you feel so good."

He keeps one arm wrapped around the leg that's over his shoulder. With his free hand, he drives two fingers in and out of her. I can hear the wet noises from where I'm standing, and my god is it hot.

Tension builds in Cora's body, visible to me as her shoulders bunch up and her fingers tighten around Ezra's curls. Her standing leg is shaking, and it looks like she's barely hanging on for dear life. A low moan leaves her mouth, guttural and loud.

Is she gonna come already? *Damn, Ezra.*

When Cora cries out, the sound echoes through the graveyard. If anyone's within earshot, I'm sure it's creepy as hell. But for us, it's . . . well, it's everything the three of us have ever wanted.

Ezra pushes Cora higher as she comes on his tongue, lapping at her until she pushes his head away. He tries to dive back in, but she shakes her head.

"Too sensitive, Ezra. Need break. One . . . one minute."

He obliges, pressing a kiss to her stomach. They stay like that, both of them panting, until Cora has caught her breath.

Standing, Ezra maneuvers her leg so it's wrapped around his torso. Then he bends his knees, guiding his cock until he's nestled deep inside of her. They both moan.

When he grabs her ass, moving to pick her up, Cora frowns.

"Ezra, what—"

"I'm fucking you against this cross, Moonflower. Nothing you can say will change my mind."

Her eyes widen, and she swears under her breath. And then she wraps her arms around his neck, and he lifts her so she can lock her ankles behind his back. He presses her to the cross and thrusts into her, making her cry out.

"Cora, fuck," Ezra grunts. He continues pounding into her while she clings to him, burying her face in his neck. "No. Look at me. I want to see you."

She whimpers, straightening so he can watch her. Sloppily, he slams his lips to hers. Their kiss is nothing more than the suppressed want and desperation they've felt for each other for years.

He pulls away, keeping his gaze locked on her. "Shit. You look so beautiful like this."

It's almost like his words set off a chain reaction. Cora's body convulses as she comes with a cry. And then Ezra groans, slamming into her one more time before he follows her.

"Oh my god," she whispers once they've both come down. "Ez, holy shit. I almost never come like that."

He nuzzles the side of her face. "That's about to change if I have anything to say about it."

She snorts, rolling her eyes, but she's smiling.

Gently, Ezra lets her down. He keeps an arm around her waist to steady her since she looks like she's ready to fall over. Then he peers closer at the cross, reading the inscription.

He laughs, pointing to the ground. "We just fucked over a priest's grave."

Cora groans, leaning against him. "Definitely going to hell."

He kisses the top of her head. "As long as you're there, it'll be heaven to me, Moonflower."

. . .

Once we get home, Cora showers, and then Ezra crashes on the couch with his head in Cora's lap. Hellraiser plays quietly in the background—it's tradition that we always watch it on or around Halloween—but Cora and I aren't paying attention to it. Instead, I'm trying to memorize the way every inch of her skin feels against my lips. Which, I've gotta say, is hard since Ezra is sleeping on her.

After a long kiss, Cora pulls away from me. Her eyes are earnest and somber as she says, "How have you been, Wild? Like, how have you *really* been?"

Hearing her ask makes my heart beat a little easier. Even while she was pushing us away, she was always there to listen when we needed her. She just wouldn't let us be there for her in return. But now, it's different. She's still the one asking how I've been, but this time, I know she'll give me an honest answer if I ask the question back.

"I've been okay," I say. "Tired and overwhelmed. And . . . worried, I guess."

"About?"

"The future, mostly." I stare at the TV, not watching the movie but not looking at Cora either. "My parents aren't the most supportive of me freelancing."

"But you like it, right? And it's working?"

"I love it. God, Cora, I love it so much. I just don't fit in a classroom. But this? It works for me. And I'm helping so many kids click with math."

Grinning, she squeezes my arm. "You're good at making it make sense."

"Yeah. But it's just . . . not very stable, you know? The company could drop me at any time. And I have to figure out health insurance and all this other shit. Part of me wonders if it's not worth it."

Cora chews on her bottom lip for a minute, thinking. "But a normal job could do the same thing, right? Fire you at any time?"

"I guess so."

"And it doesn't sound like being in a classroom would make you very happy."

"It fucking sucked."

She sighs, leaning her head on my shoulder. With one hand, she's absentmindedly running her fingers through Ezra's curls. Her other ends up on my thigh. "Being an adult is scary."

"It is."

I didn't realize she has more to say until she continues.

"But it sounds like you have a chance to do something that makes you happy, Wild. And it can't hurt to try, right? Especially if . . ."

This time, she doesn't go on.

"If what?" I nudge her, gently enough it won't disturb Ezra.

"I mean—the three of us, we're together. So hopefully we'll live together after graduation, right?" She looks up at me questioningly.

"I'd like that."

"It'd keep living expenses down," she says. "Which would be helpful for all of us. And that way if you end up having to find something else, you could rely on us for a little while."

"That's true." I hadn't thought of that. Why would I? The three of us being together is so new.

"And the thing is, it *is* working right now," Cora says. "So why give up on it just because it could fall through? *Anything* could fall through."

Except us. I'll make damn sure of that.

"That's a good point," I mutter.

"I just want you to be happy," she says. Then she glances at Ezra. "Both of you."

"We want *you* to be happy, Cora." My lips feather across her temple. *You deserve so much more than you've let yourself have.*

She doesn't respond, still gazing at Ezra. His features are relaxed, and for once he doesn't look like he has the weight of the world on his shoulders.

I snake an arm around Cora, and my heart overflows when she relaxes into me. It's been a long time since the three of us sat around together, and I've missed it so much. Having her body pressed against mine is a feeling that'll never get old.

"This is gonna work, right?" she asks quietly. "Us."

"It's worked for years. Until it didn't."

She winces, and I realize too late how bitter I sounded.

Even while she was pushing us away, I knew she cared. But that doesn't mean it didn't hurt like hell. The three of us need each other. And without Cora, both Ezra and I were a little lost.

We have her now, though.

"Sorry," I mutter.

"No, you're right. I fucked things up horribly. You and Ez are the two people I care about most, and I let myself fade from your lives all because I was scared. I know you guys said I don't have to keep saying it, but Wild, I'm s-"

"Don't."

But she shakes her head. "I hurt you for years. *Years.* That pain isn't going to disappear overnight. It wasn't fair of me to do. Especially without any explanation."

"I don't care." I stroke her cheek. "You're all I've wanted for so long, Cora. You aren't the only one who didn't speak up."

"But I'm the only one who shoved you away," she whispers.

"Doesn't matter. We shouldn't've let you do it for so long. I don't know why it took me so long to do this in the first place. But it'll never happen again. I told you, Moonflower. You run, I'll chase. You hide, I'll find you. You leave, I'll drag you back."

"I'm not going anywhere. I promise, Wild."

"Good," I murmur, leaning in and kissing her. "Now tell me how you've been. I want details."

The lights from the movie bounce off her skin as she tries to formulate an answer. Eventually, she releases a long breath. "I've been pretty miserable."

"Yeah. I know."

She snuggles into me more. "School is fine. A bit overwhelming, I suppose. Having Brooke, Liling, and Imani has been nice. I click really well with them. It's not the same as being with you and Ez, though. Emotionally, I've been . . . okay, I guess."

"No more lies, Moonflower," I say. It comes out gently yet firmly, and this time I'm able to sift out the bitterness.

She swallows. Pauses. Then, "I cry myself to sleep a lot. Quietly, because I never wanted Matt to hear. And it makes me feel so lonely, but then I'll tell myself that I deserve it for keeping you and Ez at arm's length. And then that makes me cry even more because I miss you, but I feel like I don't deserve this." She gestures from me to Ezra. "Like you two deserve better."

Clenching my jaw, I bite back the immediate response that pops into my head. Chiding her won't make her believe me. I need to come at this from a gentler, more patient angle. That's what Cora has always needed. Kindness with a hint of logic.

"What makes you think you won't be enough?" I work to keep my voice even and open.

"Because there's only one of me. And I . . . I hurt you both."

"You've been forgiven for the latter," I say, pressing a kiss to her hair. I'll remind her however many times she needs it. "As for the former, there's only one of you, but there's three of us."

"I'm not *that* bad at math," she grouses. Then she frowns. "Or maybe I am. I don't get what you're saying."

"Ez and I. We don't just have you. We have each other. Always have, always will. Just because we aren't romantically or sexually attracted to each other doesn't mean we aren't life partners. We are. And Ezra and I will always be there for each other the way we're there for you and you're there for us."

Cora's brows furrow as she listens. After a minute, she says, "I've never thought of it like that before."

"But you did. It's how you thought of us before yesterday, and you never thought you weren't enough then."

"That's different!"

I shake my head. "I've never been able to find an end to your love, Cora. You've always had enough for me and Ez, just like he's always had enough for us and I've always had enough for you two. That won't change just because we're acting on our feelings."

She opens her mouth to protest, but then she snaps her mouth shut. My logic is sound. I've got her, and she knows it.

"That makes sense," she says grudgingly.

"And *you*—" I squeeze her as I say it, "—are worthy of all the happiness the entire universe has to offer. You're not selfish for wanting to love two men, Cora. It's going to be harder on you, if anything. We're both pains in the ass."

She groans. "Don't I know it."

"Jokes aside, my point still stands. It's not selfish of you. If anything, it's the opposite. And it's not selfish to want our love. You've had it since we were kids."

Her eyes glisten with tears. I kiss her to try to distract her, but when I pull away, her cheeks are wet.

"Hey," I murmur, swiping my thumb over her cheeks. "What's going on in your head?"

"I love you," she says, her voice breaking.

"Fuck." I wrap my arms around her as best I can in our position. "I know that, Cora. I know."

"I don't want you guys to go home tomorrow, Wild." She curls her fingers into my shirt, burying her face in my chest.

"I know." Kissing the top of her head, I wonder if it would be too unhinged to make her come home with us. I know the answer immediately—she needs to stay here. To finish out school and to spend more time with her new friends.

Still, I'm a little worried. Five hours isn't that long, but what happens if she needs us? Like, quickly? Then all of a sudden five hours is a really long time.

And what if something happens with Matt while we're at home? What if he tries to break in or something? I don't know him well enough to make a good judgment on if he'd do something like that. He didn't protest much yesterday, but that's because he had me and Ezra threatening him. What happens when he knows we're gone?

"If Matt bugs you, I need you to let us know," I say lowly.

She sighs. "He texted me while we were . . ." Her cheeks turn bright pink. ". . . in the graveyard."

My whole body tenses involuntarily. "What did he want?"

"I don't know, really. He said that it wasn't fair that I kicked him out like that. That I should let him move back in. I don't think he got the implication that I'm with you two now."

Shit. "Was he on the lease?"

"No. So he can't take it up with my landlord." She bites her lip. "I'd say it was a horrible thing to do, but he has plenty of friends he can stay with. He's crashed with them on occasion before. Or he could get his own place."

"It wasn't a horrible thing to do." My voice comes out dark and cold. "He treated you like shit. More like a mother than a partner."

"Trust me," she says tiredly, "I know."

For another couple minutes, I hold her in silence. I want to stay up all night and talk. To catch her up on everything she hasn't been around to hear about. To learn about the ways my beautiful Moonflower has changed over the past couple years.

But we're all tired, and I want to make the most of tomorrow. Especially if we have to deal with Matt in some way.

Standing, I offer my hand to Cora. "Let's get some rest."

Easing herself out from under Ezra, she grabs onto me, and I pull her up.

"I don't want to leave him out here," she whispers, staring down at him with a soft smile on her features. Then she leans over him, shaking his shoulder.

He stirs with a groan, slowly blinking his eyes open. "Hmm?"

"Let's go to bed, Ez."

It takes him a minute to wake up enough to walk, and then we head into the bedroom hand-in-hand. We end up the same way we were last night, with Cora settled in between us and our arms draped over her.

"I love you guys," Cora murmurs once the lights are off.

"Love you, too," I reply.

Ezra says something that's entirely incomprehensible, and I smile. We know what he meant.

There isn't a single thing in this world that could make us stop loving you, Cora Grimm.

Chapter Eleven

Ezra

In the morning, I wake in Cora's bed even though the last thing I remember is falling asleep on the couch. My confusion is momentary, stolen away by the beautiful, large brown eyes staring at me.

There's something strangely vulnerable about realizing someone watched you wake up. With Cora though, it doesn't weird me out. It fills my head with warm, fuzzy thoughts that remind me of nights spent looking up at the stars on my parents' roof.

With a deep noise that's the best *good morning* I can manage, I pull her into me. I love the feeling of her softness molding to my hard edges. There's something so comforting about it. So right.

One of her hands rests on my chest, and the other finds its way to my back. With a tiny smile, she runs her fingers up and down my spine.

Perfect. This is perfect. Not only do I get to wake up with Cora, but I have her to myself all morning. I hung out at the coffee shop yesterday so Cora and Wilder could have some alone time together. And today, it's my turn.

Nuzzling my face in her neck, I breathe in her sweet scent. For years, it's been one of my favorite smells.

The mattress shifts, and then Wilder's arm is bumping against mine as he drapes it over Cora's side. He spoons her, kissing her hair with a sleepy smile.

"I think I've died and gone to heaven," Cora mumbles. "Or I'm having the longest, hottest, sweetest dream."

"It's real, Moonflower," I say, pressing closer to her body.

Wilder only stays in bed for a minute before getting up and throwing on clothes. "I'll see you guys later. Have fun."

I laugh when he throws me a wink. He knows exactly what we're going to do. But first, I just want to spend some time with Cora. I've craved connecting with her emotionally, and I'm not passing up the last chance I'll have before we head home.

"I'm gonna make us coffee," I say after I hear the front door close. "Come out when you're ready."

I have to crawl over her to get out of bed. As I do, I plant a kiss to her forehead, letting myself hover over her for a second. She looks beautiful like this, with her hair all messy and her eyes still half-closed.

"My pretty Moonflower," I mutter, kissing her on the cheek this time.

After a stop in the bathroom, I head to the kitchen to find that there's coffee already brewing. I shoot Wilder a quick thank you text before rummaging through Cora's cabinets. When I find her mugs, I pull out the two I was hoping she still had.

One is black with a cute, smiling ghost on it. It's the first mug she bought for her apartment. The other is white with two crows sitting on a branch and text that reads, "Attempted murder." Years ago, I saw the second one online and immediately bought it for her. It matches her horrible sense of humor perfectly. As I predicted, she loved it.

As I'm pouring creamer into her mug, Cora enters the kitchen. I immediately abandon her coffee. Sweeping her into my arms, I capture her mouth in a slow, sweet kiss. She tastes like toothpaste and feels like heaven.

She beams up at me. "I love mornings with you."

"After we're graduated, you'll never have to spend one without me," I say.

The reminder that we're leaving today causes her smile to fade for a moment. But then I kiss her again, keeping her present. I want to make the most of this morning.

After finishing her coffee, I fix my own. When I look back to her, she's perched at her little table by the window. She's watching me with a content look in her eyes, sipping from her ghost mug.

She looks perfect. Her T-shirt barely covers her ass, and whenever she bends over, I can see the navy blue fabric of her panties. The morning sunlight illuminates her hair, almost casting her in some sort of glow. It's the type of image you wish you could engrave into your memory forever. So real, so un-posed. Yet it's one of the most beautiful sights I've ever seen.

She always has been, though, hasn't she?

"I want to draw you." I don't make a conscious effort to say the words. They just fall from my mouth, almost like she pulled them from me with an unspoken spell. "Please?"

Hope sparks in her eyes. "Of course, Ez."

Before she moves, I snap a picture of her in front of the window. My phone does nothing to capture the stunning image before me, but it'll have to do.

She laughs. "What was that for?"

"I want to remember this. Forever."

Her blush spreads across her cheeks as she finishes her coffee. Then we abandon our empty mugs in the sink and I lead her back to her room.

"On the bed," I say, searching through my bag for my sketchbook and pencils. "Oh, and take off your clothes."

She hesitates with her fingers on the hem of her shirt. "Naked?"

"I want to see every detail of your body, Moonflower. Every dip, every curve, every scar. It's perfection to me, and I plan on doing nothing less than immortalizing it on paper."

The tension leaves her shoulders, and her gaze softens, meeting mine. Then she pulls her shirt over her head and steps out of her panties.

"Beautiful," I murmur. I drop my stuff on the chair I brought in from the kitchen and move to her. My lips skirt over her shoulders, down her arms, and then to her fingertips. Then I bend, kissing her full stomach before gently biting one of her breasts.

"Ezra," she whispers.

I pick her up and toss her onto the bed with a grin. "I've wanted to draw you like this for a long time, you know."

Cora's blush deepens. "I always wished you would ask."

It's going to happen a lot from now on, if I have any say in it.

Settling in the chair, I flip to a fresh page in my sketchbook. The sunlight is hitting her skin in the most perfect way. She looks . . . *fuck*, she looks almost edible, if that's even possible.

Cora lounges on the bed, propping her head up on one hand. A mischievous grin takes over her face.

"Don't say it."

She giggles.

"Don't. you. dare."

"Draw me like—"

"CORA GRIMM YOU SHUT YOUR FUCKING MOUTH RIGHT NOW."

She burst into a fit of cackles, holding her stomach and kicking her legs.

"You think you're so funny," I grouse.

"I doooooo!"

Rolling my eyes, I settle back in my chair. "Hold a position or I'm not going to draw you."

With a gasp, she settles down. "How much time do we have?"

"As much as we need. Wild understands."

I sketch her form lightly, focusing on the shape of her body. The details will come later. Right now, I just want to get her general position down. There's no way I'll have the patience to finish the whole drawing this morning, but I can get enough down that I'll be able to finish the rest later.

As her form appears on the paper, I say, "Tell me what you've been up to, Moonflower. I want to know what's been going on in your life."

"Not much, honestly," she says. "School has taken up a lot of my time. Plus working as a nurse's aide. But I like some of the people I work with, so that's nice. Still tiring."

I nod, silently urging her to continue.

"Making friends has been nice, though, even if it took me a while to get a hang of it. Liling, Imani, and Brooke have been really supportive. They were all friends before, but I don't feel like the odd one out, you know?"

"That's good, Cora. I'm glad."

Do I wish she would've relied on us for support? Of course. But I can't change the past. All we have is right now and whatever our future holds.

"And you?" she asks quietly. She squirms, rubbing her thighs together. My pretty Moonflower is getting impatient.

Good. I want her soaked and desperate by the time I'm done with this drawing.

"You heard some of how I've been. But other than that, things are going okay. Mom and Dad are more supportive of me being an artist than they were originally."

She grins. "That's awesome."

"Yeah. Now I just have to, you know, actually draw."

Biting her lip, she nods. She doesn't try to offer advice or solutions. She just listens as I continue talking about the projects I abandoned. Everything has been too much. Even now, I'm wondering if I'll be able to finish this drawing when I come back to it another day. The inspiration will be gone, and it'll probably pull me into a bad mood because she'll be five hours away.

By the time I'm done talking, she looks worried, so I give her the best smile I can manage. "I'll go to the doctor's appointment, Cora. Even if I try not to, there's no way Wild would let me miss it. And I'll . . . I'll talk to my doctor about getting on meds or something."

She nods. "And I'll always listen when you need me to, Ez."

"I know."

Once the general sketch is done, I can't wait any longer. Cora's naked body is too tempting, spread out on the bed and begging to be touched. Besides, I don't want her to keep worrying about me. That's not how today is supposed to go.

Abandoning my sketchbook and pencils, I crawl on top of her. I immediately regret not taking my clothes off first, but I'm not leaving her. So I kiss her, covering one of her breasts with my hand and squeezing.

"Not fair," she protests, tugging at my shirt until I help her get it over my head. Then her hands run over my chest.

Cora has touched my bare chest plenty of times. We used to go swimming almost every day when we were kids, and Wild and I loved throwing her in the water. But this is different. Now, her touch burns, like she's branding me and making me hers.

I have been for years.

One of her hands slips into my sweatpants and boxers. When her fingers wrap around my dick, I groan into her mouth. Never in a million years will I get enough of this. But somehow, I force myself to pull away.

"I want to tie you up."

Her eyes light up with curiosity and desire. "Really?"

"God yes. Is that okay?"

She moans just from the idea. "I thought you'd never ask."

As I grab my ropes from my bag, I slide off the rest of my clothes. Cora's gaze rakes over me greedily, further spreading the fire in my veins.

"Let me know if it gets uncomfortable," I say.

I pull her to the edge of the bed and have her bend her knees. She watches silently as I first work on her right leg, starting at the ankle with a bowline tie. Then I wind the rope around her thigh and calf, binding them together and carefully tying each hitch on the way back down.

"Oh," she murmurs, shifting slightly.

"You okay?"

"Yeah. I . . . I like it."

"Not too tight?"

She shakes her head.

"Good." I kiss the inside of her knee.

As I work on doing another spiral futomomo on her left leg, Cora's breathing gets heavier. A cursory glance in between her legs tells me she's even wetter than she was before.

"I can't wait to fuck you," I say, finishing with the rope before stepping back to look at my work.

Cora has herself propped up on her elbows. The second I move away, she instinctually closes her legs. I yank them open again.

"Uh uh. These thighs, Cora. They were made to be wrapped around my head. But today, I want them spread wide open."

She bites her lip bashfully, and it's the sweetest, most adorable thing I've ever laid my eyes on.

My knees hit the floor. For a second, I just gaze at her, spreading her legs more to get a better look. "So pretty," I whisper.

She whimpers as my breath hits her skin, and then again when I part her gently. Her taste coats my tongue, ripping a guttural moan from my chest.

"Ez," she breathes.

"Hands, Cora."

"What?"

"Hands. In my hair. Now."

She lays back, and then I feel her fingers grabbing onto my curls. She can't prop herself up anymore, so I can't see her face, but I'm perfectly fine with the trade off.

I lick her from entrance to clit before delving into her. The little gasp she makes is exactly the reaction I was hoping to pull from her. She clenches around my tongue before I pull out and flick her clit gently.

"Oh my god, Ezra."

When I pull away, her fingers tighten in my hair, and it makes me grin. "You're such a desperate little thing."

"It feels . . . it feels so good, Ezra. Please do it again."

I oblige. How could I not? I've thought of this exact moment so many times. Stopping would be the last thing I could ever want.

Every moan that leaves her lips goes straight to my dick. I stroke myself slowly—can't help myself—as I circle her clit with my tongue.

"Fuck," she whispers.

All I want to do is savor her. But I need to be inside of her, too. So I work her to an orgasm, slipping a finger inside of her when she starts to tense. Apparently, adding the slightest bit of pressure is all she needs, because she explodes. Her back arches, and her legs strain against the ropes as she screams. It's a beautiful sound, although it's concerningly loud. Still, I wrench as many cries from her as I can before pulling away.

"Christ, Cora. Your neighbors are going to think I'm murdering you."

She groans weakly. "Fuuuuuck."

"Maybe try to keep it down just a bit?"

"I'll try," she pants. "But damn, Ez."

I don't give her long to recover. I can't. So I position my dick at her entrance, pausing there. "I don't want to be gentle with you, Moonflower. I want to make you come so hard you cry. I want to leave bruises on your pretty skin. Tell me I can."

"Please," she whispers.

I lean forward, pinning her arms to the mattress. Then I suck on her breast hard enough to mark her as mine. She moans, arching into the sensations, and that's when I finally slide into her.

She gasps, her eyes locking with mine. I don't go slowly—don't give her a chance to adjust. No, I hold her down while driving into her so hard her eyes roll back into her head.

"Fuck," I grit out. I release her arms so I can rub her clit, and she brings a hand over her mouth to muffle her cries. "That's it. Stay quiet for me. Such a good girl."

The noises she makes are fucking everything. And when she comes again, I cover her hand with my own. She screams as she clenches around my cock, and thankfully the sound is muffled enough.

I try to hold out long enough to make her come again, but I can't. She feels too good wrapped around me. And I can't lie, the sight of her tied up is enough to undo me all by itself.

As I finish, my vision goes blank, and I slow my thrusts. "Oh Jesus fuck, Cora."

She whimpers, and I feel her fingers brushing down my arms as I come back to reality. Fuck. *Fuck,* that felt good.

For a minute, I hover over her, kissing my way down her body. Then I bite her stomach, making her yelp before I lick away the sting.

"Everything I could've hoped for," I murmur into her skin.

She sits up slowly, keeping her legs open. "How did that feel like . . . like magic? I never want to let you go home now."

"Oh, we're not done yet."

Her eyes widen. "We're not?"

I shake my head, undoing the ropes. "Absolutely not."

"But . . ." Her eyes flit to my cock. "You already came."

"Don't see how that affects you."

Once I'm done untying her, I give her a minute to stretch out her legs. Then I help her up and lead her to the chair. "Sit."

She does, and I position her so her legs are lined up with the legs of the chair.

"Are you going to tie me up again?"

"Mmhmm. Unless you'd prefer I don't."

"No, I want you to. Please."

With a smirk, I secure her legs to the chair. I tie her arms to the back, making sure nothing is too tight. She's dripping onto the wood below her, a mixture of my cum and her own. I think she can feel it, because she tries to close her legs yet again. Obviously, she can't, and it satisfies something deep inside of me.

Like this, I can have her whatever way I want her. Unless she says otherwise, of course. But our Moonflower has done nothing but show that she loves submitting to me and Wilder.

"Where's your vibrator?"

"I—my what?"

"I know you have one, Moonflower. Where is it?"

She hesitates before saying, "My nightstand."

I grab it before coming to stand in front of her. Then her eyes widen when she realizes what I'm going to do. I flick it on, and she whimpers, squirming against the ropes.

"How many times do you usually make yourself come with this thing?"

"Three? Sometimes two, sometimes four. Christ, Ez. I don't think I can handle that much more."

"We'll start with one," I say, lightly brushing it over one of her nipples. "And we'll go from there."

When I touch it to her clit, she jumps, so I bring it to a less intense speed. She starts trembling almost immediately, throwing her head back with a groan.

"Ezra!"

"You can take it, Moonflower."

"Fuck. Fuckfuck*fuck.* It's so much."

I move the vibrator from her clit, and her body sags against the chair. When I bring it back, she screams, tension flooding her body. I hold it there, clamping a hand over her mouth.

"So loud," I chide. "I told you to keep it down."

She whimpers out an apology.

My hand slides up until my fingers are covering her nostrils. She grunts against me, eyes wide.

"What, you thought I'd just let you get away with disobeying me? I don't think so, Cora."

Her gaze turns pleading as the lack of oxygen hits her.

"I'm not letting you breathe until you come. And you'd better keep it down. You won't like the consequences if you act out of line again."

I increase the speed of her vibrator, and she jerks against me. Within seconds, she's coming, her body convulsing in the chair.

Gently, I move my hand away. She doesn't scream, too focused on gulping in air to make much noise. When she finally makes one, it's a deep, guttural moan.

"Ez, Ez, I can't—*stop.*"

I shut the vibrator off, and she instantly melts. As she catches her breath, I take in the sight of her. She's a mess—hair stuck to her forehead, sweat coating her skin, the works.

One day, I'll be able to make her look like this whenever I want to.

"I can't handle more, Ez," she pants. "That was . . . shit. It was amazing, but I need a break. And potentially a nap."

"Of course." I set the vibrator on her nightstand, and then I get to work untying her. By the time I'm done, she's come down from her orgasm enough that her breathing has evened out.

I help her up, keeping my arms around her while she gains her footing. Gently, I kiss her, needing this moment to last a little longer.

"I should probably shower," she murmurs, leaning into me.

"I'll come with you."

She shakes her head against my chest. "You've seen my shower, right?"

"Mmhmm."

"There's not enough room for both of us."

"There is."

"But only one of us can be under the water at once. Whoever isn't will be freezing!"

"I'll deal," I say, dragging her into the bathroom. I turn on the shower, grabbing a couple washcloths. "I'm not absolutely destroying you unless I get to care for you afterward, Moonflower. It's nonnegotiable."

"Okay," she whispers.

It's tight in the shower, and I'm a little cold, but it's worth it. I wash Cora's hair, and then I scrub her body and gently clean in between her legs. She's not used to it, which makes me wonder what kind of sex life she and Matt had, but I don't ask. To be honest, I don't want to know. The thing that matters is that she's with us now.

Once Cora is done, she gets out of the shower, and I clean myself before following her. When I step out of the shower, she's dressed and waiting with a towel in her hands. She wraps it around my body before pulling me into a kiss.

"I love you," she says against my lips.

"I love you too, Moonflower. So much."

For a second, I let myself stare at her. She's wearing a black T-shirt dress paired with a couple necklaces she's had for years. One is a sterling silver death's head hawkmoth pendant that hangs low, and the other is a black velvet choker with an anatomical heart dangling from it.

They're distinctly *her*. She struggled a lot with wanting to fit in when we were in high school. Those necklaces were the first things she ever bought that matched her style, not anyone else's.

"I'm glad you still have these," I murmur, brushing my fingers over the cold metal.

She grins. "So am I."

In Cora's room, I get dressed while she puts the chair back in the kitchen. Her phone buzzes on the nightstand, and I grab it, figuring it's Wilder. But it's not. It's Matt.

I don't even pause to think. I just take the call, placing Cora's phone to my ear. "What the fuck do you want?"

Matt grunts in confusion. "Why are you answering Cora's phone? Wait. Have you guys been in town all weekend?"

"So what if we have been?"

"Have you been staying with her? Is that why she hasn't been answering her phone?"

"She hasn't been answering because you're not worth her time," I reply flatly.

Anger ignites in my chest. Worry follows closely behind. We leave later today, but not if Matt is bugging Cora. People do shitty things when they're pissed. I'm not abandoning Cora if there's a chance Matt isn't going to leave her alone.

"Well, I'd like to talk to her."

"I'm sure you would."

"Seriously man? Who the hell do you think you are? Haven't you guys barely talked for, like, three years?"

"Hey," Cora says from the doorway. "Who're you talking to?"

I turn to look at her, and my expression must clue her in.

"I can hear her," Matt says. "Let me talk to her."

"What does he want?" she asks nervously.

"You're not talking to her," I say, keeping my gaze trained on Cora. "In fact, once we hang up, you're going to delete her number from your phone. Then you're going to forget about her, and you're never laying eyes on Cora ever again. Got it?"

"What the hell are you gonna do about it?" he says, laughing. "You live five hours away."

"Fine," I say coldly. "You want to do this the hard way, then we'll do this the hard way."

I hang up, still staring at Cora. She's twisting her fingers around her curls, shifting from one foot to the other.

"What are you gonna do?"

"Make sure he leaves you alone."

"I don't think he'll do anything," she says, but her tone is unconvincing.

"If there's even the slightest chance, I'm not risking it. Wild will feel the same way. I don't want you to have to worry about him harassing you."

"But it's not like you can do anything," she says. "You guys are going to be back home. If he tries something, then . . ." She shrugs.

Placing her phone in her hands, I lean my forehead against hers. On Friday, I was jealous when I saw Cora's friends at the Halloween party, but now I couldn't be more grateful that she's not alone. "Then I guess it's a good thing you have people here you can count on, Moonflower."

Chapter Twelve

Cora

When Wilder gets back, we eat breakfast while we catch him up on the phone call. As Wilder listens, his shoulders tense up, and his fists clench at his sides.

"We're not heading home until we know he's going to leave you alone," Wilder says, tucking me under his arm.

I relax into the warmth of his body. I don't think Matt will do anything more than be a nuisance or an inconvenience, but I still feel safer knowing it'll be taken care of. Still, I'm a little lost on what they're planning on doing.

"How?"

There's silence for a second. Then Wilder asks Ezra, "You thinking what I'm thinking?"

"Considering how they acted at the Halloween party, I'd say it's a safe bet they'll help."

"Who?" I ask. Ezra mentioned my friends, but Imani, Liling, and Brooke couldn't do much. Unless they mean . . .

"Blaze looked like he'd do anything for Brooke. Same with DeAndre for Imani. And I don't know about that Ryan guy, but he was certainly watching Liling for most of the party. I bet he'd help out if it meant impressing her."

"Help out *how?*" I pull away from Wilder to look at his face, but I don't find many answers in his expression. "What are you going to do?"

Wilder shrugs. "Threatening him got him out of your apartment. Don't see why it wouldn't work again. Those three guys seem intimidating enough."

"You have no idea," I mutter. Blaze and Ryan work in private security. And DeAndre is an actor who's starred in a lot of action movies. I've seen his home gym—it's intense.

"Can you get me their numbers?" Wilder asks me.

"I . . . I guess, yeah." Pulling out my phone, I go to text the girls to ask, but a notification stops me.

Matt: I'm coming over once they've left. We need to talk.

My phone is at the right angle for Wilder to read over my shoulder. He lets out a low growl. When he tries to grab it from me, I hold it away from me.

"Cora!"

"Just let me try to figure out what he wants."

Cora: We're done.

Matt: Yeah, no shit. But you shouldn't've done it like this.

Cora: What do you want?

Matt: A fucking apology, for starters.

"That," Wilder says, jabbing at my phone. "That right there. *For starters.* I don't like that."

I'd argue, but I don't like it either. I don't bother replying, texting the girls instead. They give me Blaze, DeAndre, and Ryan's numbers. I find it a little odd—or maybe disappointing—that Imani is the one who gives me Ryan's number. Makes sense since he's in charge of security for DeAndre and Imani, but I was hoping something happened between him and Liling on Friday.

After I give their numbers to Wilder, he pulls on his leather jacket and steps outside to make a couple calls. I'm still a little lost on what exactly they're planning on doing, but I'll make him tell me before anything happens.

"Hey. You okay?" Ezra says. He steps in front of me, tilting my chin up with two fingers.

I shrug. "A little worried, I guess."

"There's no need to be." His voice is gentle and soothing, and I let it calm the anxiety welling inside me. "We'll take care of you. And while we're gone, we'll make sure you have people looking out for you."

"I just . . . I feel a little stupid. I never should've let him move in when he asked. The cheaper rent was nice for both of us, but he's a horrid roommate. I should've known better."

"Hey, it's okay. We'll take care of it."

I could probably deal with Matt on my own, but it's nice that I don't have to.

"Thank you."

"Anything for you, Moonflower."

When Wilder steps back inside, he gives us a tight smile. "All of them said they'd help you out if you need it. You just have to call."

"I could've asked them," I mumble.

Wilder raises an eyebrow. "Would you have, though? Or would you have put it off because you didn't want to be a burden?"

Ezra grimaces. "Ouch."

I hate it, but Wilder is right. I would've kept it to myself.

"Thanks," I mutter.

"Ryan seemed pretty enthusiastic," Wilder says, probably so I don't dwell on his comment for too long.

"I bet he did," I reply with a smile. He jumps on any chance to potentially get on Liling's radar. "The two of them need to stop dancing around each other."

"Seriously," Ezra says. "How long has that been going on?"

"Since this summer, I think. That's when he got the job at Grayson Security and started working on DeAndre and Imani's security team."

Wilder shrugs. "We waited years. They'll get around to it when the time is right. Now, speaking of time. We don't have a lot. Pull out your phone, Moonflower. Let's deal with this guy."

I grab my phone, and Wilder tells me what to type.

Cora: Can you meet me at the park?

Matt: Alone?

Cora: Yeah. The guys just left. Long drive home.

Matt: Fifteen minutes.

Ezra peers at the exchange. "Got it. We'll be back soon."

"What? I'm coming with you."

"No," Wilder says, "you're not."

"Yes I am!" I march past him, heading for the door, but he grabs my arm and yanks me back.

"Don't even think about it."

I give Ezra a pleading glance, but his lips are pressed into a thin line. *Shit.* I was hoping he'd take my side on this. Fine, then. I'll just have to convince them both.

"You want Matt to leave me alone, right?"

"Obviously," Wilder grits out.

"Then he needs to understand I'm on board with this. If he doesn't get that *I* want him out of my life, he won't respect it."

"We weren't planning on giving him much of a choice," Ezra says.

"Well, I'm coming anyway."

Thankfully, they don't try to stop me. It's not like they'd let Matt hurt me. And now that it doesn't matter if he calls me *nitpicky* again, I have a few things I'd like to say to Matt.

It only takes a couple minutes to get to the park. It rained last night, so everything is wet and cold, which leaves the place empty.

I convince Wilder and Ezra to hide behind some trees before Matt gets here. If I can smooth things over with him myself, I'd prefer to take that route.

When he shows up, he spots me the second he gets out of his car. With an angry look, he stalks across the wet grass until he's a few feet in front of me. "What the hell, Cora? What's gotten into you?"

I smirk. "A couple things."

Matt ignores me. "Do you know what they did? They *broke in*, and then they pushed me to the ground, and then they made me clean the bathroom. It was weird. And fucking humiliating."

Shit, I already forgot about that. I don't bother hiding my smile as I say, "Yeah, apparently you do know how to clean. That *is* weird."

His nostrils flare. "It was a shitty thing of you to do. We could've talked it out. Broken up civilly. But this was downright unfair."

With a sigh, I say, "None of it should've gone down like this, I agree. They shouldn't've kicked you out without warning, and I'm sorry for that. And, let's be honest, you and I should've broken up months ago." I reach into my pocket, pulling out a wad of cash. "Here."

"What the hell is this?"

"You already gave me your rent money for November. I'm not gonna keep it from you."

He snatches it from me. "Perfect. I'll give it to Jack. I'm rooming with him for the rest of the year. But seriously, Cora. You're really choosing those violent assholes over me?"

"Don't pretend you care. The only thing they were doing was looking out for me, and that's more than you've ever done."

Fury fills his features, and he starts moving forward, but then he stops abruptly.

"Don't take another step toward her."

In an instant, I feel a hand on my arm. Wilder steps in between me and Matt as Ezra pulls me back and into his chest.

"You lied!" Matt exclaims.

"You really think I'd meet you here alone?"

"Fuck you," he snaps. "You lying b-"

Wilder punches him before he can get anything else out. Stumbling back, Matt cradles his face. Before he can swing back, Wilder kicks him in the stomach, toppling him.

"Let me be clear," he growls. "You're never coming near Cora again. You see her on campus? Walk the other way. Hear she's gonna be somewhere? You'd better make sure you aren't there. She's always deserved better than you. And you're gonna stop being a pain in her ass by *leaving her the fuck alone.* Got it, buddy?"

As he stands, Matt rolls his eyes. "What are you gonna do about it? It's not like you two can stick around for the rest of the semester."

"You know Cora's friends?" Wilder asks, crossing his arms.

"Of course I do."

"Then I'm sure you've met Blaze and DeAndre. Probably Ryan, too." Matt's face pales.

"That's right. If they hear about you stepping out of line, they'll come for you. And Ezra and I will too, the soonest we can. So tell me. What are you going to do?"

Matt glares at the three of us, shaking his head. "I can't believe this."

"What are you going to do?" Wilder asks again, his tone more forceful this time.

"Leave her alone," Matt mutters, backing away.

"That's right. And if you don't, you'll get a lot worse than that." Wilder gestures to his face. "Now get the hell out of here. I never want to see your face again."

We watch him retreat to his car. Once he's gone, Wilder turns to me. "You okay, Moonflower?"

I nod. "Thank you. You . . . you didn't have to punch him for me."

"I certainly wasn't about to let him insult you."

Wilder kisses me, holding my face tenderly. Ezra keeps his arm around me, refusing to let go. I'm so wrapped up in them that for a minute, I forget they're heading home soon.

"I don't want you to go," I whisper to neither of them in particular.

"We're not," Ezra says, nuzzling his face in my neck. "Not yet, at least."

Relief fills me. If I don't have to face the fact that they're leaving, I can pretend they're staying forever. "Kiss me," I tell him.

He does. It starts off gently, but it grows heated within a few seconds. Ezra's tongue slips inside my mouth, and his grip on me turns hard and demanding.

"Fuck, Moonflower. I just had you, but it wasn't enough." He nips at my bottom lip. "I'll never get enough of you."

Wilder chuckles. "I'd say we could fuck you in the woods, but it's too damn cold out here."

If Ezra's expression is any indication, it physically pains him to pull away from me. He grabs my hand and pulls me to the car. "Then let's get her home."

Since we took my car, I head for the driver's side, but Ezra grabs my keys and tosses them to Wilder before dragging me into the backseat. He has my flannel off before Wilder has even started the car.

"Ez! What are you doing?"

"Not wasting a damn second with you, that's what."

Ezra kisses me again, holding my head in a firm grip that I couldn't get out of even if I wanted to. He shoves my back against the car door, pushing one of my legs off the seat to make room for himself.

"In the car?" I ask with a surprised giggle.

"I'd take you anywhere I could." His lips finally leave mine, trailing across my jaw and then down my throat. He sucks on the base of my neck.

"That's gonna bruise," I say, arching into him.

He slips his hands under my shirt. "Don't pretend you don't like it when I mark you, Cora."

"I . . . wasn't," I say breathlessly. "But it'll be harder to cover up there."

A dark smile flickers over his features. "Good."

As Wilder starts driving, Ezra manages to get his head under my shirt. I'm glad he doesn't shove it up—I'd prefer if people looking in couldn't see my naked body. Pretty sure Ezra feels the same way.

Shoving my right bra cup to the side, he runs his tongue across my breast. Then he circles my nipple, getting infuriatingly close without touching it. I groan, and Ezra chuckles against my skin.

"You're insatiable," I gasp when he finally licks my nipple.

He pulls his head out of my shirt. "Mmm, and you're not? Tell me you're not soaked right now."

I groan.

With a smirk, he undoes my jeans and shoves his hand into my panties. "Just what I thought." A single finger drags some of my arousal up to my clit, circling gently.

"Oh, fuck." My head hits the cold glass of the window as tiny sparks of pleasure shoot from Ezra's fingers.

He stops, and his eyes darken when I whine in protest. "No. I want you more desperate than this."

Fuck.

Soft, sweet, and caring. Those are the words I'd use to describe Ezra. But this weekend, I've been introduced to a rougher part of him I've never seen before. So when he backs off of me, grabbing my hair and pulling me with him, I'm not surprised.

My scalp stings as he forces me to my hands and knees on the backseat. It's enough to bring tears to my eyes, but I like it—and he knows I do.

"Undo my pants, Moonflower."

His grip on my hair only tightens when I reach for his belt. I fumble with it, and then I struggle with his button and zipper, too. He gets impatient enough that he slaps my hand away and undoes everything himself. All I'm able to do is help shove his pants down his legs.

His cock pops free, inches from my face.

"Shit. Suck his dick, pretty girl."

"Pay attention to the—*fuck,* Cora."

"I'm not gonna crash. Stop your worrying."

As I work Ezra's cock into my mouth, his grip on my hair finally loosens. He lets me go at my own pace, not trying to force himself down my throat. Every groan he lets out sends pride coursing through me. Being the source of their pleasure is something I've wanted for so long.

We get back to my apartment way too soon. Ezra tucks himself back into his pants reluctantly. His chest is heaving, and he's looking at me like he wants to do a thousand terrible, wonderful things to me.

"Inside," he grunts. "Now."

The three of us hurry up the stairs. They'll have to go soon, we all know that. But if we can have one more chance to be together like this, I'm not passing it up.

Once we're inside, Wilder disappears into my bedroom for a moment. When he comes out, he kisses me hungrily, his hands wandering over my body and squeezing.

"What should we do with you?" he murmurs against my lips.

"Fuck me," I whisper. "Please. Both of you."

"You think you can take both our dicks at once, pretty girl?"

I nod.

"You think she can, Ez?"

"Mmm, I'm not sure."

"I guess you'd better prove yourself, Cora. Get on your knees. But take your clothes off first. I want to see every part of you."

Quickly, I obey, stripping and then dropping to my knees in front of them. Wilder has his jeans undone first, so I suck the tip of his cock while I stare up at him with wide eyes.

"Shit," he groans, gathering my hair in his hands. He doesn't take control, but he keeps a tight grip. I think it's a reminder that he *can* take over at any second. I may be the one working, but I'm still completely at his mercy.

After a minute, I move to Ezra's dick. Wilder keeps his hands in my hair, shoving me forward until I gag. I push against Ezra's thighs until Wilder lets me move back. They let me have a second before Ezra drives into me at the same time Wilder shoves me forward, almost like they planned it.

I gag again, and tears fill my eyes.

"That's it," Wilder says, his voice as dark and predatory as last night. "This mouth is good for one thing and one thing only."

"Such a pretty fuckhole," Ezra adds.

I whimper, choking when he pushes into my throat. It pulls a groan from both of them.

"Shit, hold on," Ezra says, pulling out. "Can I take a picture of you like this?"

I tilt my head. "Why?"

"The way you look right now. I want to draw you like this later."

A hint of nervousness curls through me. "Just for you?"

"Just for me," he assures. "I can put the picture in a password-protected folder, and I'll keep the drawing to myself. Or give it to you."

I think it over for a second, but ultimately I nod. I trust Ezra. "As long as I get to see the drawing."

Bending at his waist, he kisses the tip of my nose. "Of course, Moon-flower."

He fishes his phone from his pants pocket, lining up the picture. Just as he snaps it, I dart my tongue out to lick a drop of precum from the tip of his cock.

Another groan as Ezra stares at the picture. "Fuck, that's perfect."

I circle my tongue around the head of his dick, smiling up at them both.

He grunts. "I love it when you do that."

Locking eyes with him, I do it a couple more times before taking him all the way down. He watches as my throat bulges, trying to accommodate him. Then his fingers brush over my neck, feeling himself inside of me.

When I pull back, my eyes are watering, and my jaw already aches. But it doesn't matter. Not when I'm on my knees with both of them gazing down at me like I'm the only thing in the world that matters to them.

I suck the tip of Wilder's cock, swirling my tongue. He swears under his breath.

"The things I want to do to you, Moonflower," he says lowly. He releases my hair, stroking my chin instead.

Moaning, I take him deeper. As he pushes into my throat, I can't help but gag a little, and it makes his eyes roll into the back of his head.

I don't try to push him away. If they want me to prove myself, then I'll do whatever it takes. I want to know what it feels like to have them both inside of me at the same time. So I hum with my nose pressed into his shirt. I grip Wilder's jeans, but he slaps my hands away.

"Hands behind your back, Cora. Fuck, Ez, tie her up."

"I'd say she's proved herself. Don't you agree?"

Wilder hums. "Yeah. But I'm not done playing with her yet."

His words send an involuntary shiver through me. These two men are my best friends. Out of everyone in my life, they're the ones I trust the most. They'd never do anything I wouldn't want. But that predatory look is back in Wilder's eyes, and it makes me wonder what he has up his sleeve.

Ezra's touches are gentle as he ties my hands behind my back. He peppers my skin with kisses that send tendrils of warmth through my body. As he finishes, Wilder pulls himself out of my mouth. Then he heads into my bedroom again, returning with a candle in his hands. The flame dances as he walks—he must've lit it when he disappeared earlier.

"What's that for?" I ask, eyeing the candle. The glass is shaped into a pitcher. Like it's made for . . . pouring.

Oh god.

"*For them to make me feel pain in the most pleasurable ways.* That's what you said in your post, isn't it?"

My breath catches in my throat. That's *exactly* what I want. So I nod slowly, eyeing the candle. "What if it's too hot?"

"This one burns at a lower temperature. But if it's still too much, I'll stop."

It occurs to me that Wilder must've put a lot of planning into this trip. Every fantasy I listed in my blog post has come true because of him and Ezra. So I smile. Couldn't stop it if I wanted to. Being loved by them is the best thing that's ever happened to me.

"You ready?"

I adjust to a slightly more comfortable position on my knees. Ezra comes to stand next to Wilder, and the sight of them both looking down at me while I'm tied up makes me whimper.

"Use your words, pretty girl."

"Yes," I whisper.

Wilder blows out the candle. Then he crouches in front of me, holding the candle at an angle, slowly tilting it more and more.

I gasp as the wax hits my chest. At first all I feel is the heat. Then the pain registers, accompanied by a moan. Wilder drips more on my breast, and it's the same. Heat. Pain. Pleasure.

"You like that, Moonflower?"

I nod breathlessly.

"Let's see how you like it when you don't know it's coming," Ezra says. He grabs a scarf that's hanging on the wall by the door. Then he places it over my eyes, tying it behind my head.

"Oh god," I whisper. Like this, I have no idea when I'll feel the wax making contact with my skin.

When it comes, I jump. Wilder does it again, and then again, all at the same pace. I expect it the fourth time. My body tenses in anticipation, and I hold my breath. But it doesn't come.

Wilder chuckles. And then, after I've already relaxed, he drips more wax onto me—right over my nipple.

I moan. It hurts, but somehow it feels good, too. When I feel the pain on my thighs, I jump. Wilder slowly moves it up my thighs, getting closer and closer to my clit. But when I feel a sensation there, it's not heat or pain. It's the soft touch of his finger rubbing gently. Then his lips are on mine, and his tongue is entering my mouth, and I'm whimpering into him.

"You worked so hard for us, and you took that so well, Moonflower. I say you deserve a reward."

"Yes," I gasp when he pulls away. "Please."

His smile reaches his golden-brown eyes as he helps me to my feet. "Let's get you cleaned up first."

Chapter Thirteen

Wilder

As we peel the wax off Cora's body, her breathing gets heavier. We keep her tied up and blindfolded while we lead her into her bedroom. I think she likes it—the thrill of not knowing what's coming next.

After shedding the rest of our clothes, we have Cora face the bed and bend over it. Her upper body and face rest against the mattress. She shifts nervously on her feet, unaware of the way we're both gazing at her.

And my god, what a sight. Her generous ass is exposed and on display, and she's so wet she's actually dripping. And those thighs—full and soft and begging to be worshiped.

Ezra swears under his breath just from looking at her, and he moves forward almost like he's in a trance. He palms her ass before getting to his knees and licking her slowly. She moans into her blankets, which are still a mess from this morning.

Leaning against the dresser, I watch as Ezra works her over until she's clenching her fists so tightly I'm afraid she might hurt herself. He pulls away seconds before she comes, running his hands down her legs.

"No," Cora sobs. "Ezra, please."

"Patience," he soothes.

She groans. But then Ezra stands, teasing her entrance with the tip of his dick. She tries to push back, to take him farther, so he steps away.

"Ezra."

He grins at me. "Think she's ready?"

"Definitely," I say. Because *I'm* ready and entirely too impatient to keep waiting.

We both help Cora onto the bed. Ezra lies down on his back, and we maneuver her so she's straddling him. Only then do we let her sink down on his cock. Ezra holds her up as she starts rolling her hips, making them both groan.

"Just like that, Moonflower," he says. "Ride me like your life depends on it."

And she does. For a couple minutes, anyway. But then I push her down so she's pressed into Ezra's chest. His arms come around her while I kneel in between their legs, squeezing Cora's ass.

"Has anyone ever fucked you here?" I ask.

"Yes," she says, yelping when I smack one of her ass cheeks.

"No one else," I say, running my hand across her reddening skin. "No one but us from here on out."

She nods, crying out when Ezra thrusts up into her. "No one else."

"You have lube?"

"In my nightstand."

I grab it before settling behind her again. She jumps at the cold lube against her warm skin. "Hold still for me, Moonflower," I say as I brush a wet finger over her hole.

She whimpers when I push inside of her. Just one finger, warming her up slowly. She squirms, but Ezra holds her more tightly.

This weekend, we've wrung orgasm after orgasm out of our girl. But we're taking one more before we leave, and it'll be the most explosive one yet.

As I add a second finger, she moans, tensing up.

"Deep breaths, Cora," Ezra murmurs in her ear. He strokes her hair with one hand, keeping his other arm firmly around her. "You have to stay relaxed for us."

Cora gulps in air, and eventually, she relaxes. "Fuck," she whispers. "Ez. Wild."

"We've got you," Ezra says soothingly, slowly pumping into her again. "We've got you."

By the time I've finished prepping Cora, she's a mewling, begging mess. I could feel Ezra gently fucking her, giving her what she wants but not enough of it. He's been stringing her along, keeping her on the edge and waiting for me. And now, all I want to do is push her over.

After coating my dick with more lube, I enter her slowly. She groans into Ezra's chest as I slide in, just a couple of inches.

"Oh god," she pants. "Oh *god.*"

"Relax, Cora."

She takes a couple more deep breaths, and then I slide in all the way, trying to take my time to let her adjust.

"Fuuuuuuck," I groan. "So tight."

"Shit," Ezra breathes. Then he undoes the scarf around her head. "Wanna see you. Over here, Cora. Look at me. How does it feel?"

"So good," she cries. "Fuck me, Wilder. Please."

"Not yet. I need you to do something first."

"Anything," she whispers.

"Tell me you deserve this."

She pauses, and based on the way Ezra's expression softens, she must be looking at him. Hell, maybe she's close to tears. I can't see her face.

"You do," Ezra murmurs, stroking her face. "You deserve both of us, Moonflower." Slowly, he slides in and out of her, making her groan. "So say it."

Another pause. Then she whispers it, so quietly I almost don't hear. "I deserve this."

"Louder, Cora," Ezra says firmly.

"I deserve both of you." This time the words fall from her lips confidently.

"You mean it?" I ask.

"I do," she replies. "I promise I do. We're practically made for each other. And I need both of you. So I . . . I deserve both of you."

Ezra grins. "That's my girl."

She kisses him sweetly. Ezra doesn't try to turn it into anything else—just lets it be the soft reassurance she needs. But when she pulls away, his eyes are still full of lust.

"Wilder," Cora says.

"Hmm?"

"Fuck me. Now."

With a smile, I grab onto her hips to use as leverage. "Your wish is my command, pretty girl."

Ezra knows it's coming. So right as I slam into Cora, he shoves the scarf into her mouth to muffle her scream. She clenches around me—around both of us—as I do just as she asked. I'm not gentle or kind or sweet, but that's not what she wants.

Hearing Cora's dampened cries and knowing I'm half of the reason for them only makes me plunge into her deeper. And when she comes, her body goes limp in between us. Ezra grins as he watches her face, pulling the scarf out of her mouth after she screams again.

Fucking Cora like this feels like heaven. It's a mix of blissful sensations that threaten to make my vision go blank, so I can't imagine what it's like to have us both inside her like this. Especially when we don't stop, even as she starts to come down.

Well, until everything is too much. I didn't want to come this fast, but it feels too fucking good. There's no way I can hold back. As I finish, I grab onto Cora, barely managing to stay upright. My thrusts turn slow and shallow as I try to draw the feelings out for as long as I can.

"Ezra," she gasps after I pull out. "Ez, don't come like this."

"You want me to come in your mouth?"

"Please?"

One last time, Ezra drives into her, staying inside of her for another second. Then he nods. "Wild, help her off of me."

I do, pulling Cora up and holding her steady as she climbs off the bed. While she lowers herself to her knees, Ezra comes to stand in front of her. She wastes no time sucking on the tip of his cock. His eyes go wide as a choked groan rips from his throat.

"*Cora.*"

She tries to move her hands to grab onto his legs and whimpers when she can't. But then she moves her focus back to Ezra, taking him farther into her mouth.

"Oh, Jesus Christ," Ezra groans. "*Fuck.* I'm gonna come."

Cora takes it all, and I watch as she swallows every drop down her pretty throat. She smiles, releasing his cock with a long, slow lick.

"You're entirely too perfect," Ezra says breathlessly.

"And I'm yours," she whispers. Her eyes flit to mine. "Both of yours."

Chapter Fourteen

Ezra

I clean Cora up with a warm washcloth while Wilder gets her a glass of water. She watches me silently, rolling her shoulders since her hands are untied now.

"Do you have to go?" she mumbles.

"You know the answer to that," I say gently.

She sighs, her eyes full of sadness. But then she smiles. "I'm really glad you guys came. That all this happened. I've missed you both so much."

"I know, Moonflower," I murmur, leaning over to kiss her tenderly. "And we'll make sure to see you as often as we can. We'll come back, or you can come home, or we'll meet somewhere in the middle. I don't want to go more than a couple weeks without seeing you."

"Two weeks max," Wilder says, coming into the bedroom with a glass of water. He hands it to Cora and strokes her hair. "I know we're all busy, but you're my top priority, Cora."

"Agreed," I say.

After a sip, she nods. "I want to put you two first. The way I always should've."

With a smile, Wilder kisses the top of her head. She already knew she was his top priority, so I think he said it to get her to say it back.

"Promise?" he says.

"Promise," she whispers.

Yep. Definitely needed to hear it.

We don't stick around for long. It's already mid-afternoon, and we still have a five hour drive. So after a lot of hugs, kisses, and a few tears, Cora walks us out.

"We'll text you when we make it back," I tell her. "Love you."

She grins. "I love you both."

Before he gets in the car, Wilder catches her in his arms. "More than the moon and the stars, Cora."

And then we go, backing onto the road while Cora blows me a kiss. I grin. She looks happy, and that makes *me* happy.

I watch in the mirror as she stands by her steps and waves. I wave back, my hand sticking out of the window. My heart aches, but that's okay. This is only temporary. It doesn't matter that we're driving away because we'll be back. And in the meantime, she's in our hearts, and we're in hers. *Our Moonflower.*

Epilogue
Cora

Graduation

The sun is shining brightly outside of Westview University's auditorium. Our graduation ceremony just ended, and I'm currently posing and smiling with the girls while our parents take way too many photos. I'd be annoyed if my heart wasn't bursting.

Wilder and Ezra are here. I can't find them—my mom keeps chiding me, telling me to look at the camera—but they're *here.* I heard them cheering when I walked across the stage. All I want is to see their smiling faces. Well, that's not *all* I want. But so far, I'm getting everything I've ever dreamed of.

We all are.

"Honey, one more," my mom calls. She can't stop smiling—Mom has always been one of my biggest supporters. When I decided to become a nurse like her, she was over the moon. And when she found out I got together with Ezra and Wilder, she was so happy she cried.

Grinning at the camera, I bask in the warmth and contentment filling my heart. For years, I thought I wouldn't get my happily ever after. But now it's here, it's *here,* and it feels unreal.

I ended up getting offered a good job in Philadelphia, so the guys are moving here. Wilder still loves his writing and tutoring position, so he'll be able to work from home. His workload is much lighter now that he doesn't have school, too.

As for Ezra, he has a steady stream of commissions coming in. He ended up getting on antidepressants, and they've helped a lot. Of course, he still has his bad days—we all do—but for the most part, he's doing much better.

As our parents finally finish up with photos, Ezra and Wilder emerge from the crowd of graduates and families. My heart leaps, and I wave to them.

"Go," Imani says, nudging me toward the guys. "Don't make them wait."

With a grin, I run to them. I barrel into Ezra's arms, and Wilder joins in on the hug. Finally. *Finally.* They're both staying in town for a few days, and then I'm going back home with them to help them move. We don't have to be separated ever again.

"We're so proud of you, Moonflower," Wilder says.

"Thank you." I kiss him, then Ezra. Then I laugh, too happy to hold it in. "I love you both so much."

Wilder hands me a bouquet of flowers and presses a kiss to my temple. Ezra bashfully shoves a manila envelope into my hands.

"You'll want to open that . . . well, don't open it here."

I raise an eyebrow. And then, of course, I open it.

"Cora!"

Inside is a single piece of paper. There's no way in hell I'm going to pull it out—especially when I realize what it is.

It's a drawing of me. I'm on my knees with my tongue out, licking the tip of Ezra's cock.

"Damn," I say, looking up at him. "It's perfect, Ez."

"I'm glad you like it."

I close the envelope, making sure the drawing won't fall out, before I throw my arms around his neck. "I'll like anything you ever draw for me."

"Cora," Liling calls from where she's standing with her family. She walks over, her long black hair blowing in the wind. "Hey, my parents are taking me out to eat, and I'm gonna be busy next week. I'm not sure I'll see you before you leave."

I wrap her up in my arms. "I'm so proud of you. Proud of us."

She grins. "So am I. Have a good trip. Oh, and I'll text you with more vacation details soon, yeah?"

"Sounds good." When I turn back to Wilder and Ezra, they're staring at me. "What?"

"Nothing," Ezra says with a smile.

"What?"

Wilder shrugs. "You're pretty, that's all. Pretty and ours."

I melt into their arms, and warmth spreads through me at how nice it is to be wrapped up in them both. *This* is where I belong. This is home to me.

Thankfully, our families have all accepted me, Ezra, and Wilder being together. Hell, they've been accepting in general. Even Wilder's parents have come around to trusting him to know what's best for his career. It took a couple long talks and some more explaining, but they got there eventually.

"C'mon, pretty girl," Wilder says, grabbing my hand. "We wanna say hi to your parents. Then we should all get food or something. I'm hungry."

I groan. "Me too. And I want to put on more comfy clothes."

Ezra hums, looking me over. "If I have a say in it, you won't be wearing anything for the rest of the day. After we're back at your apartment, anyway."

"Ez! Don't say stuff like that within earshot of my parents!"

Leaning in, he murmurs in my ear, "Fine, I'll whisper it. Once we're home, I'm tearing this thing off of you, tying you up, and having my way with you until you're begging me to stop."

I bite my lip as heat spreads across my cheeks. "You're insatiable," I squeak out.

Wilder laughs—I'm pretty sure he heard what Ezra just said to me. "For you, Moonflower? Always."

THE END.

Acknowledgments

I had a lot of help writing Moonflower. It wouldn't be nearly as great if it wasn't for everyone who gave me feedback and pointed out my blind spots.

To my alpha, beta, and sensitivity readers—Lo, Alexia, Zoie, and Alyx. You all are, quite literally, the BEST. I loved reading your comments, and your thoughts helped make Moonflower *much* more well-rounded. Thank you so much.

To everyone who gave me your opinions on the original cover—Rachel, Aspen, Alexis, Dina, Maycie, and Yolanda. It looked a lot better thanks to you guys. To Melissa, who designed the current cover, you're a gem. The cover turned out better than I ever could've imagined.

And, of course, thanks to my partner for introducing me to Pinhead and for helping me come up with the Frankenstein/Dracula joke. And, you know, for making me laugh all the time.

About Elira Firethorn

Thanks so much for reading Moonflower!

I've been writing since I was a teenager. Creating different storyworlds and characters was my absolute favorite pastime (okay, okay, coping mechanism). I've always loved romance, especially dark romance with a little suspense sprinkled in, so it's no surprise that it's what I ended up writing.

If you'd like to stay up to date with my latest writings and adventures, you can check out my website elirafirethorn.com or follow me on Instagram, Pinterest, and TikTok @elirafirethorn.

Also By Elira Firethorn

Dark Luxuries Trilogy

Deepest Obsession

Twisted Redemption

Darkest Retribution

Dark Luxuries Epilogue

Ruthless Desires Series

Blissful Masquerade

Perfect Convergence

Undying Resilience

Wretched Corruption

Cruel Betrayal

Made in the USA
Las Vegas, NV
11 March 2024